D.E. STEVENSON
THE MUSGRAVES

Born in Edinburgh in 1892, Dorothy Emily Stevenson came from a distinguished Scottish family, her father being David Alan Stevenson, the lighthouse engineer, first cousin to Robert Louis Stevenson.

In 1916 she married Major James Reid Peploe (nephew to the artist Samuel Peploe). After the First World War they lived near Glasgow and brought up two sons and a daughter. Dorothy wrote her first novel in the 1920's, and by the 1930's was a prolific bestseller, ultimately selling more than seven million books in her career. Among her many bestselling novels was the series featuring the popular "Mrs. Tim", the wife of a British Army officer. The author often returned to Scotland and Scottish themes in her romantic, witty and well-observed novels.

During the Second World War Dorothy Stevenson moved with her husband to Moffat in Scotland. It was here that most of her subsequent works were written. D.E. Stevenson died in Moffat in 1973.

D1600902

NOVELS BY D.E. STEVENSON
Available from Dean Street Press

Mrs. Tim Carries on (1941)
Mrs. Tim Gets a Job (1947)
Mrs. Tim Flies Home (1952)

Smouldering Fire (1935)
Spring Magic (1942)

Vittoria Cottage (1949)
Music in the Hills (1950)
Winter and Rough Weather (1951)

The Fair Miss Fortune (written c. 1938, first published 2011)
Green Money (1939, aka *The Green Money*)
The English Air (1940)
Kate Hardy (1947)
Young Mrs. Savage (1948)
Five Windows (1953)
Charlotte Fairlie (1954, aka *The Enchanted Isle*, aka *Blow the Wind Southerly*)
The Tall Stranger (1957)
Anna and Her Daughters (1958)
The Musgraves (1960)
The Blue Sapphire (1963)

(A complete D.E. Stevenson bibliography is included at the end of this book.)

D.E. STEVENSON

THE MUSGRAVES

DEAN STREET PRESS

A Furrowed Middlebrow Book

FM82

Published by Dean Street Press 2022

First published in 1960 by Collins

Cover by DSP

ISBN 978 1 915014 49 8

www.deanstreetpress.co.uk

CHAPTER ONE

"WHY are you so upset about it, Esther?"

The words startled her for she had thought Charles was asleep; she turned her head and looked across the room to the big bed and saw his eyes gazing at her inquiringly, his bright blue eyes with the crinkles of ready humour at the corners.

It was a large room, well proportioned and beautifully furnished; the windows faced west and Esther was sitting at the window so that she could see her sewing . . . but the light was fading fast for it was an afternoon in November.

"You can't see to do your sewing," added Charles.

"I could, really—until a few moments ago," she told him. "The light goes so fast now. I was just sitting here looking at the trees."

The trees in Highfold Park were worth looking at; they were oaks and beeches, flaunting their autumn finery in the last rays of the sun. Above them was the clear cold sky and a few racing clouds. Up there it was windy, but the garden was so sheltered that the leaves fell slowly and gently, settling upon the lawns in carpets of glowing colours.

"It's nearly your tea-time," said Esther gathering up the pieces of peach-silk material of which she was making a petticoat for Delia's birthday, folding them hastily and putting them into the work-bag.

"There's no hurry," he told her. "Come and sit on the bed and talk to me."

Esther did as he asked, perching lightly upon the end of the bed and taking his hand in hers. It was a very thin hand—far too thin and far too white—with long tapering fingers.

"That's better," he said, "I can see you properly now. Tell me why you're worrying about it."

"About what?"

"About Margaret and Bernard Warren of course."

"How did you know?" she exclaimed in surprise; for indeed it was surprising that Charles should know—or have guessed—what was happening. Charles had been in bed for weeks and she had been careful to keep him as happy and peaceful as she could.

"I keep my ear to the ground," replied Charles. He chuckled and added, "You aren't very good at keeping secrets, Esther—at least not from me—but of course I've known you for twenty-five years, haven't I?"

"Yes, but Charles—"

"And Margaret is in love. That's obvious. I've been in love myself—for twenty-five years—so I ought to know the symptoms."

"She hasn't said anything to you!"

"Not a word. But you haven't answered my question: why are you so upset about it, Esther? It was bound to come, sooner or later. When you've got three pretty daughters you can't expect anything else."

"But Margaret is far too young!"

For a few moments there was silence and then Charles said, "You don't like him, do you? I wonder why."

Esther could not answer. She did not really know why she disliked Bernard Warren and she wanted to be absolutely fair. Perhaps it was only because she hated the idea of parting with Meg . . . and if so it was not a proper reason.

"You haven't heard anything against him, have you?" asked Charles in sudden alarm.

"No," she replied. "It's just—he seems too old for Meg. He's so—so solemn. Meg likes fun—and I can't imagine them having fun together. I don't know what Meg sees in him."

Esther thought of him as she spoke . . . the tall dark solemn man with the rugged features and the slight stoop. He was by no means the Prince Charming that Esther had envisaged for her precious Meg.

"I think you're wrong," declared Charles. "Bernard Warren may not be particularly attractive to look at, but he's good and sensible and sound—and he's kind. Kindness is important—especially in a husband. Don't you agree?"

"Yes, of course," said Esther. She could not say more because of the lump of misery in her throat. Charles had always been kind—the kindest person in the world—but he had been gay as well. Although he was so much older than she was he had been full of fun. They had laughed together at silly jokes, and they had shared the great sorrow of their lives when their little son, Philip, died.

"Bernard Warren is all right," said Charles.

"But is he right for Meg?"

"Oh, I grant you I would rather he had chosen Delia, but he hasn't, and I don't really blame him."

"Delia is the eldest."

"Yes, she's the eldest," agreed Charles with a sigh.

This was another aspect of the affair which was worrying Esther. Delia was the eldest. Delia was being rather unpleasant about 'Meg's young man'.

Charles had been watching his wife's expressive face. "So there's trouble, is there?" he said. "I suppose it's natural, but honestly, Esther, you worry too much. Try to sit back and leave things to take their course. You can't do a thing about it."

This was good advice, but difficult to take. Of course Esther had always hoped that the girls would marry (no mother worth her salt would wish her daughters to remain single) but she had taken it for granted that Delia would be the first to leave the nest (Delia who had always been a little difficult, who had asked a little more than the others and given a little less), Delia first and then Margaret and lastly Rose, the baby, who had made her appearance somewhat unexpectedly when the Musgraves had believed their family to be complete.

2

Esther thought of all this, and then, for some reason that she could not have explained, she thought of Walter. Perhaps it was because he also was a member of the family— if he were still alive.

Walter was the only child of Charles Musgrave's first marriage and almost as old as Esther herself. Walter was on the point of leaving Harrow when Charles and Esther became engaged; he was sitting his exams and made this an excuse for not attending the wedding; quite a reasonable excuse considering that he hoped to take a scholarship and go up to Cambridge in the autumn to study medicine.

At the time Esther had been disappointed, she had even been a little hurt, but Charles had explained that Walter had always wanted to be a doctor.

"He's madly keen about it," Charles had told her. "He has a vocation, I'm sure of that. Of course it's a pity he can't come to the wedding but you understand, don't you?"

"Of course," agreed Esther. "His career must come first— it's his whole life, isn't it?—but he'll come to Highfold for the summer holidays and I shall see him then."

The engagement had been so short and it had all been such a rush that Esther had never seen Walter, but she would see him soon. It might be a little difficult at first—she realised that—but she would do all she could to win his heart. They would be friends in no time—they would have fun together—it would be delightful. Esther made all sorts of plans for the entertainment of her stepson.

"When Walter comes . . ." she said to Charles. "When Walter comes we must have some parties for him. We don't want him to find it dull. We could have picnics, couldn't we? We could go over to Stratford. Perhaps he would like to have a friend to stay. When Walter comes we must—"

"Perhaps it would be better if he didn't come," said Charles uncomfortably.

"Not come!" she cried in dismay.

"He could go abroad with the Mainwarings, and come here later on when things have settled down."

Even that did not warn her. "Oh Charles, but this is his home. I'm sure he would rather come to Highfold. We mustn't be selfish! He must never feel pushed out! You and Walter have been everything to each other for years—haven't you?"

"Yes, that's just it."

Even then she did not understand.

But Walter had not been in the house twenty-four hours before she realised her mistake. It was impossible for her to make friends with him; he had determined not to be friends and the more she tried to charm him the more he withdrew into his shell.

Unfortunately Esther was very young and inexperienced; instead of leaving him alone, she tried to draw him out. She asked him what he had been doing, and what he would like to do. She asked about his friends at Harrow; she asked him what he liked to eat. Walter answered in as few words as possible. He was grave and 'correct'; he was polite to the point of impertinence.

They had arranged to go for a picnic together, and as it was a very fine day there seemed to be no excuse for not going. They sat on a bank and ate their lunch. Esther tried to make conversation but after a few brave efforts there was nothing more to say, so they sat there in silence.

"Better go home now," said Charles, looking at his watch.

Walter rose at once. He helped to pack the basket and carried it to the car.

"Perhaps you would like to sit in front with your father," suggested Esther.

"No thank you," replied Walter coldly.

They drove home without another word.

Several days passed but the situation became no better. There was no contact to be made. Walter never spoke unless he was spoken to. He sat through every meal in silence. Charles and Esther tried to speak to each other, but they found it impossible to speak naturally and soon they gave it up in despair. The three of them were bound together by convention, but divided by a sheet of ice.

Perhaps it was Charles who suffered most, for he was deeply in love with his young wife. He saw her laying herself out to be friendly and pleasant. He saw her getting snubbed. He saw her relapse into silence, wounded, miserable, disappointed.

When Esther realised that nothing she could say or do could mend the situation she made the excuse of a headache and went upstairs to her bedroom in the hope that when she had gone the other two would talk to each other, but apparently this was no use at all. Whether she was there or not Charles could make no contact with his son.

"He's like a block of ice," said Charles when he came up to bed. "He's full of resentment. He's more angry with me than he is with you. I wish he were a few years younger—young enough to be whipped. That's what he needs."

"Oh Charles—no! Poor Walter!" exclaimed Esther incoherently. "We must be patient."

"Patient! Haven't we been patient?"

"Yes, but he's jealous. It's miserable to be jealous. Please be patient, Charles. Perhaps it will be better tomorrow . . ."

She was weeping now. He took her in his arms and she clung to him shaking all over with sobs. "It's all my fault," she whispered. "I've been terribly, terribly stupid . . . I didn't understand . . . you shouldn't have married such a little idiot . . ."

Esther had said, 'perhaps it will be better to-morrow' but it was worse. Esther had said, 'please be patient' but Charles had come to the end of his patience. That evening, after dinner, the impossible situation blew up.

Esther never knew the details of the quarrel, for she had gone to bed early, tired out with the day of misery and frustration. She had been lying there for nearly an hour when Charles came up—in fact she was half asleep.

"Well, that's that," said Charles. He spoke quietly, but his eyes were blazing furiously and his face was as white as death.

"What—" began Esther—and then found she could not go on.

"I've told him," said Charles. "I've told him I won't stand his behaviour a moment longer. Neither I will. I've been patient—because you asked me—but it's intolerable. I can't bear it."

Charles had begun to walk up and down the room.

"I can't bear it," he repeated. "I told him so. I told him he was making our lives a hell. I said he must apologise to you—or get out."

"Oh Charles—you shouldn't!" cried Esther in dismay. "I don't want him to apologise. I only want—I only want—"

"I know," said Charles, pacing the room. "You've done your best—nobody could have done more—but it's no use. I've done my best too. I can't bear it any longer."

"Charles, come here," said Esther.

He came and sat on the bed and she took his hand in hers. There was a few moments' silence.

Presently Charles said in a calmer tone, "I lost my temper. I said more than I intended . . . but he sat there and looked at me . . . with that queer sort of smile on his face . . ."

Esther had seen 'that queer sort of smile' on Walter's face.

"I know," she whispered. "You've been *very* patient. Oh Charles, I'm so sorry about it all. What can we do?"

"Perhaps things will be better now," said Charles, returning the pressure of her hand. "Sometimes it's better to bring things out into the open. At any rate they couldn't be worse, could they?"

"No."

"He'll come round in time."

"Yes, of course."

"It's just a matter of time. When he goes up to Cambridge and gets settled into his work he'll be more sensible. Meanwhile it's better that he should go away—better for him and better for us. He can fly over to Nice and join the Mainwarings. We'll talk it all over quietly in the morning. Things always look brighter in the morning."

But on this occasion things did not look brighter in the morning.

Walter had packed a suitcase and gone and he had not joined the Mainwarings at Nice. They found a letter on the chimney-piece—a few lines hastily scrawled. Charles read it and threw it in the fire.

"The young fool!" he exclaimed.

"What does he say?" asked Esther in a trembling voice.

"Says he's chucking Cambridge."

"Chucking Cambridge!"

"Yes. Says he won't be beholden to me for another penny. Says he'll stand on his own feet—from now on."

"Oh, how dreadful! How dreadful! All his work gone for nothing!"

"Yes, all in a moment."

"Where can he have gone? Where can he be?"

"I don't know—nor care."

"But—but has he any money?"

"I don't know," repeated Charles.

"It's all my fault!" cried Esther. "I tried so hard—but it wasn't any use. I've ruined Walter's life—ruined it completely—and I've driven away your son! Oh Charles, what are we to do? What *can* we do?"

"We can't do anything—except wait. Don't worry too much—he'll come back. He'll find it isn't as easy as he thinks to 'stand on his own feet' and it won't do him any harm to endure a little hardship. He'll soon get tired of it and come to his senses. We shall be hearing from Walter one of these days."

"Do you think so—really?"

"I'm sure of it," said Charles.

But Charles was wrong. Weeks passed and they did not hear from Walter (he seemed to have vanished from the face of the earth) and all this time Charles never mentioned his name. This was not to say he never thought about him; of course he thought about Walter, of course he was worrying. Several times Esther broached the subject and suggested that something should be done.

"What should be done?" asked Charles in a cold hard voice.

"We should try to find him."

"How?"

"Couldn't we—couldn't we ask the Police to—"

"No, I shall do nothing. Walter knows where we are and if he wants to communicate with us he can do so. Obviously he doesn't want to communicate with us, so what would be the use of finding him?"

This was true, of course.

It upset Charles to speak of Walter so Esther ceased to speak of him.

3

Months passed—and years. Gradually Esther taught herself to forget the whole miserable business. She found it easier to forget Walter when her own babies began to arrive; she was busy and happy and her life was full of other things. Sometimes a chance remark or a paragraph in the papers would bring him to mind, but this happened less and less often . . . as a matter of fact she had not thought of him for years.

But now, sitting upon the end of Charles's bed she thought suddenly of Walter. Perhaps Charles wanted to see his son. Was there any chance of finding Walter and telling him that his father was so dreadfully ill, and asking him to come? Quite often there were SOS notices out on the wireless programmes. There had been one that very morning: 'Will John Smith last heard of ten years ago in

Battersea come at once to Birmingham where his father, James Smith, is dangerously ill.'

Ten years since John Smith had been heard of! Walter had not been heard of for twenty-five!—and anyhow, when she considered the matter seriously, Esther realised that she could not do it. She could not do it without telling Charles—and Charles would be angry at the mere idea. It was madness to run the risk of upsetting Charles.

Esther heaved a big sigh.

"Still worrying?" asked Charles. "Still thinking about Meg? You worry too much, darling. I've told you to sit back and let things take their course. If Meg wants to marry Bernard Warren we can't do a thing about it."

Esther hesitated. She had been so far away—in time and place—that it was difficult to come back to the present.

"I suppose we can't," she said slowly. "It would be no use saying anything."

"None whatever."

"If only Meg were not so young! Meg is far too young—"

"You said that before, but she isn't really too young to be married. Meg is a grown-up person and knows her own mind; Meg is twenty. You married me when you were nineteen."

"But you—were—you." She was playing with his long slender fingers, crossing and uncrossing them—and her tears had begun to fall.

"Don't cry, darling," he said. "And don't try to keep any more secrets from me. It's better to face things together, isn't it?"

There was another secret which she had been trying to keep from him but she saw that he had guessed that too. It was unlike Charles to rush his fences; it had always been his policy to 'sit back and let things take their course'. He was rushing his fences now because he knew he had not much time.

4

Esther was still struggling with her tears and wondering how to answer when the door opened and Margaret came in with a laden tray.

"Here's your tea," she said cheerfully. "I've brought yours too, Mummie. You can have it together, can't you?" She switched on the light, arranged the little table and made everything comfortable for them.

"You're looking very nice," declared Charles as she settled his pillows. "That's a new frock, isn't it, Meg?"

"Yes," admitted Margaret. "Yes, it's new. I thought I'd wear it to-night. Bernard asked me to supper—his mother is staying with him—so I thought I'd wear it. Bernard will bring me home—I shan't be late. You don't mind, do you, Mummie?"

"You see!" exclaimed Esther when the door was closed.

Charles nodded. "But let's look at the bright side. You haven't looked at the bright side, have you? Bernard Warren is settled here; he's a partner in his father's firm at Ernleigh, so he won't take Meg away. Meg might have married a soldier and gone to Cyprus. You wouldn't have liked that, would you?"

"No, but all the same—"

"And the Warrens are nice people," continued Charles. "Everyone in the district liked old Warren. He was so sound, so dependable—full of integrity. He was a very clever lawyer into the bargain."

"Oh yes, he was nice," admitted Esther. "But Bernard isn't like his father at all."

"I think he is. Not to look at, perhaps, but he has the same outlook on life—the same integrity. They wouldn't have taken him into the firm if he hadn't been pretty good value. Old Warren might have been prejudiced in favour of his son—I grant you that—but Baynes wouldn't have agreed. Warren, Baynes and Warren are known all over the district—remember that."

Esther knew all this, of course, and she knew that Charles was just talking to soothe and reassure her, but all the same she was soothed and reassured.

"Well, if you think so," she said a little more cheerfully.

"I think so," declared Charles. "And anyhow if they decide they want to be married we shall have to agree. We can't prevent them, can we?"

"No, I suppose not."

Charles paused for a moment and then added, "And we won't make them wait. We don't believe in long engagements, do we?"

Esther was silent. As a matter of fact she had been thinking that they might be induced to wait. Surely they might wait until Meg was twenty-one!

"We don't believe in long engagements," repeated Charles. "We were engaged for six weeks—and it seemed like six years."

"I know, but that was different."

"It's always different—and it's always the same," said Charles rather wearily. "In this case it will be better for everyone if they are married soon. It will be better for us and better for themselves and, above all, better for Delia. You see that, don't you?"

"Yes," said Esther reluctantly. "Yes, it's true." Charles was tired—he had talked too much—so she tucked him up comfortably and left him to rest. She knew now exactly what she would have to bear and in spite of her misery she felt more settled in her mind—more confident in her ability to bear it.

Chapter Two

1

How old you can grow in three years! It is only a fraction of time but to Esther Musgrave it seemed longer than all the rest of her life put together. In three years she had become an entirely different person—or so she felt. She looked the same of course. When she glanced at herself in the mirror she saw the same features and was surprised to discover that she looked no older. There were no grey hairs and no wrinkles, no signs of advancing age.

Esther had expected that she would never be happy again; it seemed incredible that she should be happy without Charles. But she had a natural buoyancy which kept her afloat and after a time she discovered that she had begun to take pleasure in sunshine and flowers and the song of birds—and even in food and pretty clothes. Most of all she found pleasure in her new house and every time she returned to it after a morning of shopping or a visit to friends she paused for a moment with her hand upon the green gate and looked at it with affection.

It was a small compact house; the sort of house that could be run quite easily—how different from Highfold! On either side of the front door there was a bow window, and above there were three windows. The house was of Cotswold stone and the roof fitted snugly. Over the front door was a curious device carved in stone—a horse's bridle—which gave it character. Esther had never been able to discover the reason for the device but the house was called The Bridle House, so it must have meant something to a bygone owner.

Now that Margaret was married and Rose away at school, Esther's only house-mate was Delia, and unfortunately Delia did not like The Bridle House; she sighed for the wide spaces of Highfold Park and all its amenities. Sometimes Esther herself had qualms; and waking at night in her small comfortable room she wondered what Charles would have thought of it; but, there again, if Charles had lived it might have been possible to carry on at Highfold. It was only after Charles's death that the big rambling house had become an intolerable burden; the roof had begun to leak; plaster had fallen from the ceiling in the upstairs bathroom and dry-rot had made its appearance behind the bookcase in the study. Even then Esther would never have thought of leaving Highfold Park if Bernard had not suggested it (Bernard had been appointed Executor of Charles Musgrave's Estate).

"Why not move?" Bernard had said. "Buy a small house in Shepherdsford. It would be much more comfortable for you."

"Move?" asked Esther, gazing at him in amazement.

Bernard nodded. "You could sell Highfold. You can do as you like but I'm afraid it will take every penny of your income to live at Highfold Park and keep the place in good condition. You'll have nothing over."

He paused, but Esther was silent.

"You could think about it," suggested Bernard. "As a matter of fact there's rather a nice little house in Shepherdsford village which is coming into the market. It belongs to a client of ours. Somehow I thought of you when I saw it. Of course you may not want to move, but I believe you'd be happier in a small house, easily run and not so isolated. Meg thinks so too."

"I don't know," said Esther doubtfully. She saw the advantages of course but Highfold Park had been her home for so many years that it was difficult to imagine herself anywhere else.

"Don't decide in a hurry," said Bernard. "Come and see the little house—there's no harm in having a look at it. I feel sure you would like it."

So Esther had gone with Bernard and seen the little house and had liked it so much that she made her decision then and there.

Contrary to her expectations the move was quite easy. Bernard managed everything for her without any fuss. Bernard was one of Esther's blessings, for which she thanked God every night. It was curious that she had not liked him at first—in fact she had positively disliked him. Charles had been right. She saw that now.

2

To-day, returning from a shopping expedition in Shepherdsford, Esther paused as usual and looked at her little house. It really was hers—her very own—in a way that Highfold Park had never been. She was happy here.

Now that they were living in the village Esther discovered that it was a friendly place. Her neighbours were pleasant and kind and she found herself swept into various social activities. She ran the little house (with the help of a 'daily') and she worked in the garden, so she had no time to brood. I am lucky, thought Esther, and then—for some unknown reason—her eyes were suddenly full of tears.

Esther was blinking them away when a car drove up behind her and Bernard unfolded himself and got out.

"Hallo!" he said cheerfully—and then he said, "Hallo?" in a different sort of voice.

"It's all right," declared Esther, blowing her nose. "Just silly, that's all. Take no notice."

"Not regretting Highfold?"

"I never do," she told him. "Never for a moment."

Bernard took the basket from her hand and opened the gate. "Meg is coming to tea," he said. "We're meeting here—that's the idea—she's been shopping. Could we sit on the seat for a minute, Esther? I want to talk to you."

The afternoon was warm and bright and sunny. (As a matter of fact it was the beginning of a warm bright sunny summer which was to break all records—but they did not know this).

"What a difference you've made to the garden!" exclaimed Bernard as they sat down together. "It's a delightful garden. You've put a lot of hard work into it, haven't you?"

"Yes, it's mine, you see," she replied smiling at him. "I never felt Highfold garden was mine. It belonged to old Denvers. I was allowed to walk in it—that's all."

Bernard smiled too. He said, "You like me now, don't you, Esther?"

She nodded. "Yes, Bernard. I'm very fond of you. You've been very good to me . . . and you've made Meg happy."

"I've tried to," said Bernard gravely. He hesitated as if there were more to say—and then continued in a different tone, "I want to speak to you about business, Esther. As you know we have advertised Highfold Park to sell or let but so far without success. We've had no reasonable offers at all. We've had to spend a good deal of money on the place, what with one thing and another—and now there's the roof."

Esther knew about the roof.

"I'm afraid that's going to be rather an expensive business," declared Bernard. "There's no need to be alarmed; we'll just have to be careful."

"Careful?" she asked. "You mean I'm spending too much?"

"Perhaps a little," he told her. "But don't worry, we'll sell Highfold one of these days and then it will be all right."

She nodded. As a matter of fact that sort of thing did not worry Esther. She worried about her family and when people she loved were ill or miserable, and she worried when she found herself inadequate to meet the demands of life, but not about money nor possessions.

"I'm sorry about it, Esther," continued Bernard. "Perhaps I shouldn't have advised you to move. Perhaps we should have waited until we had sold Highfold."

"No," said Esther firmly. "I couldn't have borne it a moment longer. Highfold was getting me down. First one thing happened and then another—and the house felt so cold and empty without Charles—and if I hadn't bought The Bridle House someone else would have bought it—that horrid man with the yellow teeth and the bristly hair!"

Bernard smiled. His mother-in-law amused him a lot.

"Well, you know he would, Bernard," said Esther smiling in return. "He wanted it very badly and if you hadn't got in first with my offer he would have bought it straight off."

This was perfectly true. The horrid man with the yellow teeth and bristly hair had been circumvented rather cleverly by Bernard. Bernard had forgotten all about him but Esther's description evoked him so vividly that Bernard saw him quite distinctly for a moment.

"I could economise," continued Esther thoughtfully. "If Delia would help a bit more in the house we shouldn't need a daily help."

"Delia wouldn't," he replied. "It would mean you had to do everything yourself and it would be far too much for you." He hesitated and then added, "I've been thinking out a plan."

"What sort of plan?"

"You may not like it. The fact is some of the trees in the park are getting old. I got a forestry expert to look at them and he says they ought to come down."

"Oh Bernard!"

"I was afraid you wouldn't like it, but I think we should take this man's advice."

"But that would cost a lot of money, wouldn't it?"

"No, it wouldn't. You see we could sell the timber for a good price and use the proceeds to repair the roof. The trees will have to come down sooner or later and if we wait too long the timber will be rotten. We'll get nothing for it at all. I really think the trees should be felled, Esther."

"Well, if you think so," said Esther reluctantly. "I hate the idea, but it seems the sensible thing to do."

"I'm sure it's the sensible thing to do," declared Bernard with a sigh of relief. Obviously he had expected his mother-in-law to be much more difficult to persuade.

"You see I trust you," she explained. "And I *do* know a little about trees—Charles taught me. Trees mature, like people, and then they begin to deteriorate. It seems dreadful to fell a tree—I shall never forget how miserable I was when the beech in the corner of the paddock came down—but one shouldn't be sentimental about trees."

"Don't go near the place till the job is finished and it has all been cleared up," suggested Bernard.

"No, I shan't," she agreed.

Having settled this matter satisfactorily Bernard moved on to another subject. "I've had a letter from Walter," he said.

"Walter!" exclaimed Esther in astonishment.

"Yes, Walter Musgrave. The letter was addressed to his father, and came to my hands because I'm the executor of the estate."

"Bernard, how amazing!"

"Yes, it's amazing."

"I can hardly believe it. I thought he must be dead."

"I thought so too," agreed Bernard. "Your husband told me the whole story before I married Meg. He wanted me to know about it. I felt certain then that Walter must be dead."

The mention of Walter's name had raised so many unhappy memories in Esther's mind that for a few moments she could not speak. She had not thought of him for years but now suddenly she saw him—the tall thin boy with the long legs and arms and the thin white face. She remembered the misery of those days at Highfold Park when she had tried so hard to make friends with Walter—and failed. She remembered Charles's grief at the loss of his son, a grief all the more bitter because he refused to speak of it.

Bernard had been watching Esther's face. He said at last, "I'm afraid this has upset you dreadfully."

"Yes," she replied. "Yes, it has. It seems silly to be upset—after all these years—but it was the worst thing that ever happened to me. Even little Philip's death wasn't quite so frightful . . . it was a great sorrow but—but Charles and I bore it together. . . ." She hesitated and then added, "But it's no use being miserable about 'old unhappy far-off things', is it Bernard? Why has Walter written? Does he want money?"

"Apparently not," replied Bernard. "It's quite a short letter—just says he's been knocking about but is now settled in a good post near Cape Town. Says he's sorry he didn't write before—"

"Sorry!" cried Esther. "He ought to be sorry!"

"He wants news of the family."

"I don't think I *could* write to him," Esther said slowly. "I mean I wouldn't know what to say, or how to say it. I still feel angry with him for the way he hurt Charles, and it would be no good writing angrily—if you know what I mean."

"Yes," agreed Bernard. "Of course you're angry—that's only natural—but after all he's a member of the family and his letter ought to be answered. Perhaps you'd like me to write. I could write a semi-business letter and tell him all the news. How would that do?"

Esther accepted the offer gratefully.

CHAPTER THREE

1

MARGARET came across the grass with her shopping-basket on her arm and the two people who loved her looked at her with pleasure. She was good to look at; not really pretty, perhaps, for her features were irregular: her nose too short and her mouth too large. In fact, strictly speaking, she was the least good-looking of the family. Her charm was in her expression, in the serenity of her widely-spaced blue eyes and her rose-leaf complexion. Best of all there was a warmth in Margaret which won her many friends.

"Hallo, you two!" she exclaimed. "Lazy people, sitting here talking! I don't suppose you've made tea—or anything."

"I was just going to—" began Esther contritely.

"Don't worry. I'll do it," said Margaret . . . but instead of doing it she stood and looked at them and smiled. "I like to see you talking," she told them. "Gossiping like a couple of old women with your heads close together!"

"Talking business," declared Bernard. "Talking about roofs and trees and things."

"Gossip," retorted Margaret. "Just gossip, that's all."

"I'll make tea," said Esther, beginning to rise.

"No, don't move. I'll do it in a minute. But first I've got a piece of news for you. The new people are moving into Fairways. What do you think of that?"

"Oh, how exciting!" exclaimed Esther.

"They've got lots of money and very good taste, Mrs. Winter is very keen on music and goes in for Bridge Parties in a big way."

"Mrs. Winter?"

"Yes, that's the name."

"Who told you all that?" asked Bernard.

"Nobody," replied Margaret, raising her eyebrows with an expression of innocence. "I don't listen to gossip. I just saw the furniture van, that's all."

"Quite simple," nodded Bernard. "They were carrying in the furniture of course."

"Yes. There was a mahogany sideboard with a brass rail and beautiful brass handles—I wouldn't have minded having it myself—and there was a double bed with a tapestry back and one of those very fat spring-mattresses. There were half a dozen bridge tables and a grand piano and several chairs which looked like Chippendale. They may have been copies, of course, but they looked to me like the real thing—I didn't like to hang about and gaze—and there was an enormous dressing-table with a glass top and three mirrors." She paused and looked at her husband in surprise. "What's the joke, Bunny?" she inquired.

"Are you sure you didn't—hang about—and gaze?"

"Oh, I see! Well, as a matter of fact I didn't—so there! The furniture van wanted to know the quickest way back to the main road so I had to stop and explain. I couldn't help seeing the furniture, could I? I'm not stone blind."

"Obviously not," Bernard agreed. "And I suppose you saw a label with WINTER written on it—or did the furniture van tell you?"

"Neither," retorted Margaret. "That's puzzled you, hasn't it Bunny? I just happened to hear one of the furniture men saying to the other that they were to treat the piano with care and not dump it down. 'Mrs. Winter sed as 'ow we was to treat the pi-anner as if it was full of eggs'. Those were his exact words," declared Margaret with a chuckle. "So I drew the obvious conclusions."

They were all laughing now . . . and all three went into the little house to prepare the tea.

2

"I wonder what they're like," said Esther as she filled the kettle. Her interest in her new neighbours was not mere idle curiosity; in a small place such as Shepherdsford it is vitally important to have congenial neighbours.

"She's very good-looking," replied Margaret without hesitation. "Only a very good-looking woman could bear to see herself in three mirrors. Oh, I forgot! She's got a child—a boy about nine years old."

"Don't tell me!" exclaimed Bernard. "It was a bicycle of course."

"Of course," agreed Margaret. "That's easy. A new one, painted red, with a shiny lamp on the handlebars."

So far they had stuck to facts but when they had wheeled the tea-trolley into the sitting-room and had settled themselves comfortably the two young Warrens gave rein to imagination and endowed Mrs. Winter with an elegant figure, an extensive wardrobe and a lurid past.

"She's pale and languid," said Margaret. "She's the sort of woman who sits on a sofa with a far-away expression in her eyes. Men fall for her like ninepins."

"She wears trousers," declared Bernard.

"Oh no!" cried Margaret. "Not trousers, Bunny. She wears tea-gowns."

"Trousers," said Bernard firmly. "They suit her. She has long elegant legs."

It was all in fun, of course, but to Esther the character and appearance of her new neighbour took definite shape—as if I had seen her! thought Esther in surprise.

The boy also took on reality and became flesh and blood. With no more to go on than a bicycle Margaret and Bernard decided that he was an only child, completely spoilt by his widowed mother. Bernard was positive that he sang like a cherub and Margaret agreed.

"'Angels ever bright and fair'," said Margaret nodding.

"What about Mr. Winter?" asked Esther.

"There isn't a Mr. Winter," replied Margaret. "Call it feminine intuition if you like—I know there isn't."

Bernard said masculine intuition told him the same.

"There's no such thing as masculine intuition," objected Margaret.

"Why not?" asked Bernard. "Why should the male of the species be denied a sixth sense?"

Esther listened indulgently. She had taken no part in the absurd discussion; they were too quick for her; they were too clever. She and Charles had had fun and silly jokes together, but not like this. She suddenly remembered saying to Charles that Bernard was "too solemn for Meg". She had been wrong about that too. The mere fact that the joke was carried on with an appearance of solemnity made it a great deal funnier. Occasionally Meg broke down and giggled but Bernard preserved his gravity throughout.

The odd thing was that Esther had never heard them talking nonsense before—had not known they could talk nonsense—but that was because she had rarely been alone with them. Usually Delia was there, and somehow or other one did not talk nonsense when Delia was there. . . .

"Where's Delia?" asked Margaret. It was as if she had read her mother's thought, and perhaps she had, for thought-reading is a frequent occurrence between people who are in accord with one another.

"She has gone to a meeting of the Dramatic Club," replied Esther. "They're choosing a play, so I don't suppose she'll be home for ages."

"Let's hope Delia gets a meaty part in it!" exclaimed Bernard. "The trouble with Delia is that she hasn't enough to do."

"She does a lot," objected Esther, who felt obliged to stick up for her absent daughter. "She's on the committee of the Women's Institute and collects for all sorts of different charities."

"She ought to get a job of some kind," said Bernard.

"What kind?" asked Margaret. "I can't see Delia in a job."

"I suppose she ought to have trained for something," said Esther vaguely. "There was some talk of it when she left school, but she didn't seem interested in anything special. We thought she would marry."

"You can't depend on that. Every girl ought to have some sort of training . . . and that reminds me about Rose. What does Rose want to do. She's leaving school, isn't she?"

Esther nodded. "I want her to stay on another year, but she won't. Rose is no scholar, I'm afraid."

"She has other things," said Margaret quickly. "Rose is a darling—and so pretty—she's sure to marry. Meanwhile you could have her at home and teach her to cook and to manage a house, couldn't you Mummie?"

Bernard said nothing. He thought this was quite a good plan—as far as it went. A year at home would do no harm but after that Rose would have to be trained for a useful and profitable job. He was not going to sit back and see Rose turning into a second Delia if he could help it.

3

Whilst Bernard had been thinking—and making plans for his young sister-in-law—Margaret and her mother had been talking of domestic matters.

"How is the new girl doing?" Margaret wanted to know.

"Oh, very well," replied Esther. "She's a great improvement on Cynthia—but I knew she would be of course; Lady Steyne recommended her highly. Her sister has worked at Underwoods for years and once or twice when Daphne was ill Flo 'obliged' in her place. They're really nice people which makes a difference. I went and saw the mother; she was a cook before she was married and she still looks like a cook."

"What does a cook look like?" asked Margaret.

"I can tell you," said Bernard, chipping in to the conversation. "I remember my mother's cook quite well. She was plump and good-natured and as neat as a new pin. That's right isn't it, Esther?"

Esther laughed and admitted that Flo's mother was just like that, and the cottage they lived in was as neat as its mistress—polished and shining.

"Mrs. Bloggs is a great talker," continued Esther. "I didn't have to ask any questions at all. She told me all about her daughters—she only has the two. Daphne—the one who works at Underwoods—has never been any trouble, but Flo was a bit delicate until they took out her tonsils. The doctor said she ought to have had them out before but Mr. Bloggs doesn't hold with operations so he took a lot of persuading. I gathered that what Mr. Bloggs says goes."

"Quite right," said Bernard solemnly. "A man ought to be master in his own house."

"Ses you!" exclaimed Margaret.

CHAPTER FOUR

1

IT WAS late when Delia returned from the meeting of the Dramatic Club. Esther was preparing supper when she heard the front-door open and shut; a few moments later Delia walked into the kitchen.

"How did it go?" asked Esther.

"All right," replied Delia. "We chose a period play called *The Mulberry Coach*. It's by Jane Harcourt."

"Oh, I know! At least I know the book—very thrilling with a duel and an elopement and a highwayman holding up a coach!"

"Yes, that's it. Of course it's slightly different from the book—for one thing the heroine is called Angela instead of Agnes—but the plot is the same and most of the characters."

"Why did it take you such a long time to choose?"

"Oh, you know what it is! Everyone wanted something different. But eventually it was decided and everyone was pleased except Freddie."

"It ought to make a good play," said Esther thoughtfully. "There's so much action in it and the dresses will be very becoming."

"That's what I thought," Delia agreed. Obviously Delia was very pleased indeed with the outcome of the deliberations.

"I hope you've got a good part."

"They persuaded me to take Angela."

"Oh, how lovely!"

"There's not much 'lovely' about it," Delia declared. "It will be a frightful bore—I didn't want it—but if I hadn't taken the part they would have given it to Helen and that would never have done. She would have made a mess of it."

Esther was busy stirring white sauce so she did not reply. She wished she did not see through Delia so easily. Why couldn't Delia be natural? Why did she have to pretend she wasn't delighted at having been chosen to play the part of leading lady?

"Mark is to be Ralph; he's the hero," continued Delia. "And Helen is to be the old nurse. We haven't decided who is to be Giles, the villain of the piece. It's a difficult part and we haven't got anyone really suitable, but I dare say we shall be able to find someone."

"Who is to be the old father?"

"Tom Blake. It's rather a nice part. Sylvia Newbigging is to be the innkeeper's daughter."

"Oh yes," said Esther. "I remember. She's in love with Giles, isn't she? She nurses him when he is wounded in the duel—at least that was in the book."

"It's the same in the play," nodded Delia. "And Freddie Stafford is producing as usual. It took ages to persuade Freddie. He wanted a modern play. He kept on saying there were too many characters and we hadn't enough members in the club. He said we ought to have understudies for the principal parts in case somebody got appendicitis . . . but who wants to be an understudy?" said Delia scornfully.

"Who wants to have all the trouble of mugging up a part and then not having the chance to play it?"

"I know, but still—"

"Then Freddie said it would cost a lot of money to put on a period play; we should have to hire scenery and costumes and the club couldn't possibly afford it. That's nonsense because we would get it all back—and more besides—from the sale of tickets."

"If it were well advertised in the local papers."

"Yes, that's what I said, and the others agreed. People are sick and tired of modern drawing-room comedies but they'll all take tickets and flock to see a play like *The Mulberry Coach*."

It was not often that Delia talked like this. Usually she was inclined to silence. Esther welcomed the change; she wondered why it was that Delia had that queer twist in her nature. If Delia could be like this, cheerful and excited with bright eyes and a pleasant flow of conversation, why couldn't she be like this more often? How much nicer it would be for her relations! How much nicer for herself!

Perhaps Bernard is right, thought Esther. Perhaps Delia ought to have something worthwhile to do. Perhaps we ought to have insisted on her being trained for a job . . . and if so it's all my fault, thought Esther rather miserably.

Delia continued to talk when they sat down to supper—and Esther listened and nodded and made suitable comments. It was not until the end of the meal that she managed to get a word in.

"The new people are moving into Fairways," said Esther at last.

"Oh, that's interesting!" exclaimed Delia. "What are they like?"

Esther hesitated. She was completely muddled as to what she really knew about them and what was wild surmise . . . and it was no use trying to explain the joke to Delia, for Delia would not understand. Delia would think it silly nonsense. It *was* nonsense, of course, thought Esther, but nonsense can be very funny indeed. Esther felt sorry for her eldest daughter because of her inability to laugh at silly nonsense.

"What are they like?" repeated Delia.

Esther did not reply. Fortunately Delia took this to mean that she did not know.

"I wonder what they're like," said Delia. "I wonder if they play golf. Perhaps they would join the Dramatic Club; we need more men."

"There isn't—" began Esther—and then stopped.

"Isn't what?"

"We don't know whether there is a Mr. Winter."

"Winter? Is that their name?"

"I think so," said Esther doubtfully.

"Who told you?" Delia wanted to know.

Esther did not want to answer this question either so she rose and began to clear the table. The fact was she tried to say as little as possible to Delia about Meg and Bernard, and to Meg and Bernard about Delia. They did not get on very well and were apt to be a little unpleasant about each other . . . and Esther was aware that if she said one word more Delia would continue to pester her with questions until she had got to the very bottom of the matter. (Charles used to say that his eldest daughter would have made a fortune at the Bar).

"What do you know about the Winters?" asked Delia pursuing her mother into the kitchen.

"Nothing—really," replied Esther with perfect truth—for, after all, what did she really know about her new neighbours?

"That means you do know something. You said there wasn't a Mr. Winter. How did you know that?"

By this time Esther was not only muddled but irritated so she replied with unusual asperity, "I didn't say that at all. I said we don't know whether there is or not. It isn't the slightest use asking me about them. I've told you I don't know. If you haven't got anything else to do you can help me to wash up."

Delia took the dish-cloth reluctantly. She said, "All right. It doesn't matter. You needn't tell me if you don't want to. I suppose there's some mystery about them but I'll soon find out. I shall call at Fairways to-morrow and ask for a subscription to the Conservative Association . . . or perhaps the R.S.P.CA. would be safer."

"Much safer," agreed Esther trying to hide a smile; but she was still a little irritated so she could not help adding, "They may be Liberals or Socialists or Communists for all we know but they're sure to be fond of animals—or at least to pretend they are."

"I don't know what you're getting at," declared Delia, looking at her mother suspiciously. "Everyone hates cruelty to animals."

2

Delia stood upon the doorstep of Fairways and rang the bell. For a few minutes nothing happened. She was about to ring again—for she was not easily put off—when the door was opened by an elegant young woman with golden hair. She was wearing dark-red corduroy slacks and a pale-blue pullover—an unusual mixture of colours but very becoming.

"Mrs. Winter?" asked Delia, who had made quite sure of the name by questioning the milk-man.

"Yes."

"Oh good! I'm awfully sorry to bother you when you've just moved in, but I wondered if you would care to give a small subscription to the R.S.P.C.A."

"Oh—yes—of course," said the newcomer reluctantly. Then she looked at Delia carefully and added in a somewhat warmer tone, "Come in, won't you? I must find my bag."

The house had been redecorated, so it was natural for the visitor to exclaim in admiration.

"Oh, what a difference!" exclaimed Delia. "One wouldn't know it was the same place! We used to come here when it belonged to old Colonel Rutherford. It was such a depressing sort of house in those days: dark and dingy, with stags' heads on the walls!"

"It *was* rather awful," agreed Mrs. Winter smiling. "I wouldn't have bought it, of course. Colonel Rutherford was my husband's uncle and he left it to George in his Will. At first we thought of selling it but nobody wanted to buy it so it stood empty for years. It was just a white elephant, that's all. Then, after George died, I came down here and had a good look round and decided I could 'make it over' as the Americans say."

"You've certainly made it over!"

"Yes, there was a lot to do: there was only one small bathroom and no fixed basins—quite incredible!—and the whole house had to be redecorated from top to toe. . . ."

Thus talking Mrs. Winter ushered her visitor into a large room which had been Colonel Rutherford's dining-room and which Delia remembered as a dark cold shabby apartment hung with blood-curdling oil-paintings of battle scenes.

"Oh goodness!" cried Delia, hesitating at the door. "This can't be the same room!"

Certainly it was transformed. The walls were white, the parquet floor was adorned with a few good persian rugs; there was a divan with cushions on it, several comfortable chairs and a grand piano. A very large radiogram stood in one corner.

"I'm having this as my music room," explained Mrs. Winter.

"Oh, how lovely!"

"It *is* rather nice," agreed its owner. "Of course I'm not quite settled yet—I must get new curtains—but I'm not going to put another stick of furniture in here."

"It's perfect. I'm so glad you're musical."

"Musical? Oh well, it amuses me to strum. I can't play really well, you know—just accompaniments and things like that."

This modest disclaimer pleased Delia considerably, nothing could have been better from her point of view. "We must get you to join the Dramatic Club," said Delia. "You will, won't you? It isn't a big club, and we're all very amateurish, but we have a lot of fun. By the way I'm Delia Musgrave; we live at The Bridle House, just up the road, so we're quite near neighbours."

"How nice," said Mrs. Winter. "Yes, perhaps I might join the Dramatic Club. I've done quite a lot of acting, one way and another."

By this time they were right inside the music room. Mrs. Winter indicated a chair to her visitor and sank gracefully on to the divan. Obviously she had forgotten the R.S.P.C.A. and Delia had no intention of reminding her, or at least not at present. The animals had served their purpose in gaining Delia an entrance to the house . . . and she was the first visitor! It really was a triumph. Everyone in the place would want to hear about the newcomer to Fairways.

So far Delia did not know a great deal about Mrs. Winter, it was essential to know more.

"You've done a lot of acting?" said Delia in an inquiring tone of voice.

"One way and another," repeated Mrs. Winter casually. She added, "But I don't know if I would be much use to the Dramatic Club. I shan't be able to go out in the evenings during the holidays."

"You have several children?"

"Goodness, no! I've a young nephew coming to stay and I couldn't leave him alone in the house. To tell you the truth," said Mrs. Winter confidentially, "I'm not looking forward to his visit—I don't know much about children—but I couldn't refuse. You see my sister has just had an operation and my brother-in-law is in business so he's out most of the day. They couldn't possibly leave the child in their small flat in London . . . so I shall have to have him here until his mother is better." She sighed and added, "Christopher is rather a difficult child."

Mrs. Winter had taken a cigarette and fitted it into a long holder. She made a decorative picture reclining upon the divan. Her fair curls were slightly rumpled and her slender legs were crossed.

(Could I wear slacks, wondered Delia.)

"I'm so glad you came," said Mrs. Winter. "There's such a lot to do that I've been working like a dog all day. You're a marvellous excuse for a rest. Tell me about Shepherdsford, Miss Musgrave. Shall I like it, I wonder."

"There isn't much to tell. I'm afraid it's rather a dull little place but there are a few interesting people. We try to liven it up as best we can. There's a good golf course, and a Bridge Club—but that only functions in the winter—and there's an occasional cocktail party. There isn't a cinema, so if you want to see a film you have to drive over to Ernleigh which is six miles away . . . and then of course there's the Dramatic Club, as I told you."

"Yes, I should like to join that—if they'll have me."

"Everyone will be delighted to have you!"

"Because I'm new I suppose," suggested Mrs. Winter smiling.

"Not only that," declared Delia. She rose as she spoke for she was aware that she had made a good start with her new neighbour and it would be a mistake to stay too long.

"Oh, but you mustn't go!" cried Mrs. Winter. "You're my first visitor! You must have a glass of sherry and wish me luck."

CHAPTER FIVE

1

WHEN Delia returned home full of news she was disappointed to discover the house empty . . . and then she remembered that Esther had said she was going to tea with Lady Steyne. So she got out her copy of *The Mulberry Coach* and sat down to study it. She had known before that there would be a good deal to learn but there was a great deal more than she had bargained for.

Angela *was* a talkative young woman. She appeared in nearly every scene and prattled incessantly.

Delia was quite horrified when she realised what she had taken on for she was 'a slow study'. For a few minutes she actually entertained the idea of ringing up Freddie and telling him she could not do it after all (it will take hours and hours;

it will take weeks, thought Delia in dismay) but then, on the other hand, what joy if she could manage it! They had never asked her to play the lead before. She saw herself appearing in the attractive costumes of 'Angela'; she saw herself playing the most important role in the colourful production; she saw herself bowing to the plaudits of the audience—or curtseying perhaps! Yes, 'Angela' should curtsey.

Delia swept a slow graceful curtsey in front of the mirror in her bedroom and although she was not wearing the right sort of costume she decided it was not at all bad.

Meanwhile Esther was sitting in Lady Steyne's drawing-room drinking tea.

Esther often went to tea with Lady Steyne, for although Lady Steyne was much older than Esther they were great friends. Lady Steyne was charming, she was like a little Dresden figure, beautiful and delicate; her house was beautiful too and full of lovely old furniture. There was a peaceful atmosphere in Underwoods which Esther appreciated and enjoyed—and she liked Miss Penney who was Lady Steyne's companion. The three ladies were having tea together in the drawing-room.

At first they discussed the weather; it was worth discussing. Esther could not remember such a long spell of fine dry sunny weather, but Lady Steyne declared that it was no better than the summers of long ago.

"I hope it will continue," Esther said. "Rose is coming home and she will enjoy it."

"Dear little Rose!" exclaimed Lady Steyne. "I can hardly believe she's grown-up. Children are so sophisticated nowadays but Rose had that sweet wondering innocent look—"

"She still has it," said her mother smiling. "When Delia was seventeen she was quite grown-up; Meg was, too, in a different sort of way, but Rose is still a child. I think she should have another year at school but she doesn't want to stay on. All her best friends are leaving at the end of this term. She wants to come home."

"It will be lovely for you to have her."

"Yes, lovely," agreed Esther.

"What are her tastes?" asked Miss Penney.

Esther found that a little difficult to answer. "She's fond of games," said Esther thoughtfully. "She likes acting—she was very good as Rosalind in the school play—and she likes drawing and painting. I'm afraid none of that is going to get her very far in life but it can't be helped. People are what they are—you can't change them. Besides I wouldn't change a hair of Rose's head," she added hastily.

"No, of course not," Lady Steyne agreed. "It would be a very dull world if everyone were alike. You must bring her to tea here one day unless it would be too dull and boring for her."

"Rose would love it," said Esther. "She's never bored. She enjoys everything. . . ."

For a few minutes they continued to talk about Rose and then moved on to another subject.

"You'll call on Mrs. Winter, I suppose," said Lady Steyne.

"I suppose I must," agreed Esther. "I think Delia wants me to call. I'd really rather wait and see what she's like. I mean it's such a waste of time unless you've got something in common. Do you happen to know anything about her?"

"Only that her husband, George Winter, was a nephew of Colonel Rutherford, that's all."

"Oh, that's the connection!"

"Yes, that's the connection. When Colonel Rutherford died he left the house to George Winter. He had nobody else to leave it to."

"I can tell you a little about Mrs. Winter," put in Miss Penney diffidently.

"Can you?" exclaimed Lady Steyne in surprise. She laughed and added, "Penney knows everything. I couldn't get on without her."

Esther thought this was true. Miss Penney was no beauty, she was short and stout with a flat sort of face, pale blue eyes and sandy hair, but she was worth her weight in gold to her employer; she was absolutely indispensable—as few people are.

"Do tell me about Mrs. Winter," said Esther eagerly. "Where did you meet her, Miss Penney?"

"I met her some years ago when I was companion to Mrs. MacBrayne. Of course she took no notice of me—I mean she didn't talk to me—but I heard quite a lot about her from other people."

"Go on, Penney," urged Lady Steyne. She was aware that Miss Penney required encouragement. Indeed it was only since she had come to Underwoods that she had learnt to join in a conversation; her previous employers had not wanted her to talk but only to make herself useful.

Miss Penney thought of this and smiled. She said, "Mrs. Winter's sister, Mrs. Poulton, was a friend of Mrs. MacBrayne's. She and her husband were very keen on Bridge but they couldn't go out in the evening unless someone went and looked after their child."

"So you did," said Lady Steyne nodding. "Goodness, Penney, I never knew baby-sitting was one of your accomplishments!"

"Christopher was a dear little baby. I had no trouble with him at all," declared Miss Penney. "As a matter of fact I enjoyed going round to the Poultons' flat. I sat by the fire and read a nice book. It was peaceful and pleasant."

All this was interesting in its way, but Esther wanted information about her new neighbour. "Tell me more about Mrs. Winter," she said.

"Well, let me think," said Miss Penney. "She's tall and slender with very fair hair; her name is Eulalie—a most unusual name."

"Most unusual!" exclaimed Lady Steyne. "I've never heard it before."

"Shall I like her?" inquired Esther anxiously.

Lady Steyne laughed.

"Well, but it's important," explained Esther. "She lives so near."

"I wouldn't say she was quite your type of person," replied Miss Penney with caution. "But that's no reason why you shouldn't be kind to her. I expect she may find it rather dull. I gathered she had travelled a great deal; she was fond of travelling and had come into money from an old aunt—or some other relation. She met Mr. Winter in California and they were married out there. Mr. Winter was a very delicate man and had gone to California for his health (it is said to be a very good climate) but after they were married they came home—which wasn't very wise."

"So then he died?" suggested Lady Steyne.

"Yes. He was old, you see—much older than his wife— and suffered from bronchitis." Miss Penney hesitated and then added, "The MacBraynes used to talk about it—not very kindly."

"I suppose they said she had killed him," suggested Lady Steyne.

"Well—yes," agreed Miss Penney. "But of course it was merely a façon de parler. Mrs. MacBrayne had a habit of exaggerating—a very dangerous habit, I think."

"Lots of people talk wildly," said Esther smiling.

Her companions agreed.

Esther felt it was now time to ask after Edward Steyne, who was Lady Steyne's stepson. She asked somewhat diffidently for she was aware that he had been engaged to Lady Steyne's niece, Barbie France, and that the engagement had been broken off. Everyone in Shepherdsford had been talking about it. Some people said Barbie had behaved very badly and had 'chucked Edward' for no reason at all. Whether or not this was true Esther did not know.

"Edward has given up his post in London," replied Lady Steyne. "So he's staying with me until he finds something else to do."

She said no more about Edward, so Esther did not pursue the subject and presently she rose to go.

"I wonder if you would give me a lift?" asked Miss Penney. "I've got one or two things to do in Shepherdsford, so if it wouldn't be a bother—"

"No bother at all," declared Esther.

2

"I'm afraid this is a subterfuge," said Miss Penney as she climbed into the car. "I've got a parcel I want to post in Shepherdsford and one or two other little things to do but nothing that couldn't wait until to-morrow morning. I wanted a little chat with you, Mrs. Musgrave."

"Yes, of course," said Esther encouragingly.

Miss Penney was silent for a few moments and then she said, "I do wish Mr. Edward could get something to do. It's so bad for a young man to be idle. He had a good post in London but he didn't like it, and then he was offered a post in Kenya, but he turned it down. Unfortunately Mr. Edward has enough money to live on. It seems odd to say this is *unfortunate* but I dare say you know what I mean."

"Yes," agreed Esther.

"He has got a very comfortable little flat in Chelsea," continued Miss Penney. "And he lives there most of the time, but it's hot in London so he's staying at Underwoods, doing nothing and wasting his time. It worries Lady Steyne a lot. She doesn't like talking about Mr. Edward."

"I realised that. Perhaps I shouldn't have mentioned him, but it seemed queer not to ask."

"It was natural to ask, and I'm sure Lady Steyne wouldn't mind my telling you. It's just that she doesn't like talking about it herself. I expect you know that he and Barbie were engaged to be married. There was a lot of talk about it, wasn't there?"

Again Esther agreed.

"They were engaged," repeated Miss Penney. "And then, after a very few days Barbie realised her mistake. She felt she couldn't marry him after all. I can't tell you the reason, it was all rather complicated. Some people might think it was a small thing, but I didn't and neither did Lady Steyne. It was a matter of principle, you see."

"I see," said Esther but she said it doubtfully. She did not see—how could she?

"I wouldn't have told you this," continued Miss Penney, "but I know people are saying it was Barbie's fault and that she behaved badly . . . and I don't like it. After all," said Miss Penney earnestly, "surely everyone must agree that if you're engaged to a man and then suddenly discover that you've made a mistake and don't feel you can marry him it's better to tell him so honestly and make a clean break."

"Yes, of course," agreed Esther.

"You may have heard that Barbie has married Commander Buckland?"

"Yes, I saw it in the papers; they were married in London, weren't they?"

"But that wasn't the reason," explained Miss Penney. "I mean it was some time after her engagement to Mr. Edward had been broken off that Barbie went to Scotland and met Commander Buckland at his sister's house."

"I see," said Esther again. This time she really did 'see'. She added, "Well, I'm glad you told me. If I hear any more talk I can put people right about it. I suppose that's what you want me to do."

"Yes, that's what I want," declared Miss Penney with a sigh of relief. "You can put people right so easily—in a few words—it's much more difficult for us. You could say it was 'incompatibility of temperament' and Barbie broke it off on that account. Couldn't you?" Esther agreed that she could.

Having settled this matter satisfactorily Miss Penney changed the subject.

"Tell me about Margaret," she said. "I always think your Margaret is one of the most delightful girls I've ever met."

What mother could have resisted this bait? Esther certainly could not. The subject of Margaret and her little house lasted quite easily until they reached Shepherdsford and Miss Penney was dropped at the Post Office to dispatch her parcel.

Chapter Six

1

MARGARET Warren loved her little house. She and Bernard had designed and built it themselves on the hill overlooking Shepherdsford. What fun it had been! They had watched it go up from the very foundations; they had seen it take shape before their eyes: the walls, the roof, the charming little veranda where they had planned to have their meals in good weather. It was all exactly as they wanted it. At last it was ready—with all the labour-saving devices that the heart of woman could desire.

They had been very lucky as regards furniture, for it was just at that time that Esther was moving from Highfold Park to The Bridle House so there were plenty of 'pickings' for Margaret and Bernard.

"I don't want that bookcase," Esther had said. "And I've no room for this sofa—and you can have those chairs if you like."

So what with one thing and another the little house was furnished without any trouble at all.

There was a whole row of little houses in Richmond Terrace, all of which were newly-built and most of which belonged to newly-married couples so there was no lack of congenial neighbours. Mark and Joan Henderson lived next door and Tom and Edna Blake had a slightly larger house farther along the Terrace. At the end of the Terrace there was a very much larger house called Richmond Park, which had been built at the beginning of the century, long before any of the smaller houses had been thought of. This belonged to Colonel Newbigging, a retired Army Officer, who lived there with his son and daughter. Lance Newbigging was in the Navy, so he was seldom at home, but Sylvia lived with her father and kept house for him. Sylvia was Margaret Warren's special friend; they had known each other since they were small children and had gone to school together. Together they had endured the pangs of home-sickness and had comforted each other . . . so it was a friendship founded on rock. Fortunately Bernard and Colonel Newbigging liked each other and had a great deal in common—for one thing they were both keen chess-players—so the families fitted in well.

The Colonel's parents had lived in Shepherdsford; it had always been his home. He had known Bernard's father and Margaret's father—indeed he knew practically everyone in the district—so it was natural that when he retired from the Army he should come back to the place and settle down. He was fond of saying that he was the grandfather of Richmond Terrace, and certainly he was a good deal older than most of the inhabitants, but he was young for his age with an upright soldierly figure and a twinkle in his eye. Young people liked him and found him interesting, and he liked young people—especially Bernard and Margaret Warren.

Margaret Warren was more fortunate than many of the young wives who lived in Richmond Terrace, for her husband did not have to catch the early train to town. Bernard's office was in Ernleigh—a bare six miles away—so he could go in and out by bus or in the little car. Occasionally, if business were slack, he could return home for lunch; but business was not often slack; the firm of Warren, Baynes and Warren was well-known in the district. Bernard's father, Wilfred Warren, had built it up by hard work and ability and a delightful personality. Then, when Wilfred Warren died, the other two partners had carried on.

Some people were of the opinion that Bernard Warren was wasted in a small town like Ernleigh and would have been better advised to establish himself in London, but Bernard did not agree. He liked the country, he knew everyone for miles around and was interested in their affairs. Possibly he might have made more money in London, but money was not everything. Margaret agreed with him, she too liked Shepherdsford—and of course she was near her mother which meant a great deal.

Margaret was thinking of all this as she went about her work, sweeping and polishing and making preparations for lunch (a more substantial meal than usual for she expected Bernard home). How lucky she was, thought Margaret. Her lines were laid in pleasant places. There was only one thing missing in the little house.

Having got through her work quickly she decided there was time to clean the electric stove and she was busily engaged with this messy task when the front-door bell rang. Who could it be? wondered Margaret. Not Joan nor Sylvia of course, for they would have walked straight in. Perhaps it was a man selling things. . . .

It was a man, but obviously not the kind of man who sold things. Margaret was suddenly conscious of her stained overall, the red duster tied over her hair and the dirty gloves on her hands.

"Oh!" she exclaimed in dismay. "I was cleaning the stove! It's a frightfully dirty job. I thought it was just a man selling brushes or something—"

It was unlike Margaret to babble, but she was taken by surprise.

"You don't know me," said the man, smiling.

"No," said Margaret. "At least—I think perhaps—perhaps I've seen you before—somewhere—"

"You haven't, but you've seen someone like me. I'm a bit like my father—and yours."

She gazed at him in bewilderment.

"I'm your stepbrother, Walter Musgrave," he explained.

"Walter!"

He nodded. "Yes, Walter. Your husband wrote to me, you know."

Usually Margaret was adequate to deal with any situation (not because she was self-assured, but because she did not think of herself at all; she thought about other people) but taken thus at a disadvantage she did not know what to do. She never doubted his word for now that she looked at him she saw that he certainly bore a resemblance to her father—and his—but how should one greet a stepbrother whom one has never seen?

"May I come in?" asked Walter Musgrave.

"Oh, goodness! Yes, of course! What am I thinking of? I was just—surprised. Do come in." She tore off the overall and the duster and the dirty gloves and led the way into the little sitting-room. Luckily she had done it first, before she started on the stove, so it was beautifully clean and tidy.

"What a charming room!" said Walter. "And what a lovely view!"

"We built it ourselves," Margaret told him. "I mean we built the house—not the view."

He turned from the window and smiled at her. He had an attractive smile which made his eyes crinkle at the corners.

"Oh yes, you *are* like Daddy!" Margaret exclaimed involuntarily.

"I'm glad you think so," he replied. He sat down on the comfortable chair indicated to him by his hostess and added, "I wondered what you would be like."

Margaret would have been interested to know whether he was disappointed in her—or not—but she resisted the impulse to inquire. She was agreeably surprised in her stepbrother. He was nice, she decided. Her impression, before she saw him, had been that he was not nice at all. Certainly he had not behaved 'nicely'. Nobody could possibly say it was 'nice' to go off into the blue and vanish—and take no notice whatever of his relations for all those years.

"I know what you're thinking," said Walter gravely. "It was very wrong of me, but I hope you'll all forgive me."

"You didn't write—or anything. Why didn't you write and tell us where you were?"

"Oh, well, it's a long story. It's very difficult to explain. I doubt if I could make you understand."

"I could try to understand, couldn't I?" Margaret said.

2

The chair in which Walter was sitting was near the bay window and he was gazing out. He said, "It began when I heard that Father was engaged to be married. He wrote me a letter about it—I was at Harrow at the time. Until then Father and I had been all-in-all to each other; he was more like an elder brother than a father, he understood all my difficulties and enjoyed my school jokes. He had been at Harrow himself and when he came down for the sports and we walked about together I was so proud of him that I wouldn't have changed places with a king. We used to look forward to the holidays when we could shoot and fish and do everything together. I idolised him and I knew he had no interest in anything or anyone except me—so it really was a bomb-shell when I heard about his engagement to a young girl not much older than myself! From the very beginning I was determined to dislike her and when I went home to Highfold and saw them together it was more than I could bear.

"It seems a queer thing to say but if they hadn't been so happy together I don't think I should have minded so much—or if she hadn't been so young and attractive. To me there was something quite horrible in seeing Father blissfully in love."

Walter paused for a few moments and then continued, "She was charming to me—she set herself out to be friendly—but I was so jealous and so full of bitterness and resentment that I wouldn't and couldn't respond—and I was even more angry with Father. I won't bore you by telling you all the details—I don't like thinking about it—but we had a frightful row one evening and I decided to walk out. I decided to be independent and to make my own way in life—I decided that I wouldn't take another penny from Father—so instead of going up to Cambridge and studying medicine as we had planned I packed a small suitcase and went off on my own. I knew Father would be terribly hurt and disappointed but I wanted to hurt him because he had hurt me so terribly . . . not a very pleasant story, is it?"

"No," said Margaret gravely. "It was horrid of you, Walter, but I think I can understand."

"I was a silly fool," continued Walter. "I thought I could make my own way in the world without much trouble. I was young and strong and I didn't mind hard work; I had an exaggerated idea of my own capabilities. I worked my way to the Cape and arrived there without a penny in my pocket, and then I managed to get a job at the docks. That was hard work—a good deal harder than I had bargained for—I lived in squalid lodgings which were all I could afford. It was pretty grim. Then I got a job at a garage with two fellows who were starting on their own. Things were a bit better until one of the fellows went off with the cash and left us stranded. I did all sorts of things after that but I never seemed to have any luck, I never seemed to be able to get my head above water. At last I managed to save a bit and I went into partnership with a chap on an orange-farm. We didn't do so badly to begin with, but then we had a bad year and we hadn't any capital to fall back on—so we went bust. That meant I had to start again from scratch.

"I'm afraid this is all pretty boring for you but I want you to understand that I didn't have a very easy passage. My idea had been to make good. I intended to write to Father when I got settled in a decent job; I wanted to show him I could stand on my own legs; I wasn't going to write and tell him I was broke. That's why I didn't write."

Margaret nodded. "Yes I see; but it was a pity—"

"Of course it was a pity but I was still angry, still resentful. I was carrying a chip on my shoulder—if you know what that means. It doesn't help you in life if you go about with a chip on your shoulder; you're apt to be touchy and to fall foul of people and you don't have any friends. After the orange-farm had packed in I went back and worked at the docks (you can always get work at the docks if you're willing to take off your jacket) but it was even tougher than before.

"There was a fellow who lived in the same lodgings; he had a room just opposite mine across the passage and we were always running into each other and getting in each other's way. He was a great strong ugly bruiser of a chap—I couldn't stand him. One night I lost my wool and went for him tooth and nail. It was idiotic of course for he was twice my size. He beat me up properly and the next thing I knew I was in hospital; I was there for nearly a month."

"Oh poor Walter, how dreadful!" exclaimed Margaret.

"It was the luckiest thing that ever happened to me," declared Walter, smiling at her with his crinkly smile. "All those years I had been so busy trying to keep alive that I never had time to think things out properly. There was plenty of time in hospital to think things out. I saw then what a fool I'd been and I was pretty sick with myself.

"There was a young fellow called Hallsey in the bed next to mine; we talked to each other and I told him a bit about my experiences. One day he asked me what I was going to do when I got out of hospital and I said I didn't know. So then he said would I like a job. *Would I like a job!* I could hardly believe my ears. I knew that he and his brother owned a big fruit-farm, a fine place up country, they grew fruit and vegetables and canned them and exported their produce. It was a flourishing concern. Quite suddenly my luck had turned."

Margaret thought it was high time his luck had turned.

"Of course I had to learn the business from the bottom," continued Walter. "But I didn't mind that. I stuck into it like mad and the Hallseys were very decent to me—"

"Hallsey!" exclaimed Margaret in surprise. "I always get Hallsey's tinned peaches and things whenever I can!"

"Shows your sense," said Walter smiling. "Hallsey's are the best. I'll send you a box of all our different canned goods when I go home."

"When you go home? But—but isn't this your home?"

"Not on your life," he told her. "I'm settled there for good. I've got an excellent job in Hallsey's. They've made me manager, and I've got a bungalow of my own on the estate."

"You've certainly 'made good'," said Margaret gravely.

There was silence for a few moments and then Margaret added, "But, oh Walter, I wish you had written to Daddy! He wanted to see you when he was ill."

"I didn't know he was ill. I meant to write when I got dug in at Hallsey's but it wasn't an easy letter to write and I kept putting it off. It sounds a feeble excuse but I really was desperately busy learning the ropes—and time went by so quickly. It wasn't until the Hallseys offered me the post of manager that I pulled myself together and sat down and wrote. When your husband replied and told me Father was dead it gave me an awful shock—somehow I had never thought of that. I had imagined myself walking in to Highfold and saying I had 'made good on my own'. I see now that it was a wrong thought—altogether wrong and stupid."

Margaret was silent. She could not disagree.

He sighed and added, "Your husband wrote me a very kind letter, Margaret. Much kinder than I deserved."

Margaret had seen the letter before it was sent—in fact she had helped to compose it—but she did not tell him that.

"Very kind," repeated Walter. "It was because he seemed so kind and understanding that I decided to come and see you first—you and your husband. I want to know exactly how things are before I see the others. The fact is I'm doing well now, so I could help a bit if your mother would like to go back and live at Highfold."

"She doesn't," said Margaret. "She's ever so much happier at The Bridle House . . . and I think she has enough money, but Bernard could tell you about that."

"Do you think your mother will forgive me?"

"Mummie would think it wrong not to," declared Margaret without hesitation.

"You mean she would forgive me if I explained and told her all I've been through. You mean 'tout comprendre, tout pardonner'?"

"No, not that at all. That's muddled thinking, Walter. I know lots of people say that, but they haven't thought it out."

"I don't understand," he told her.

"But it's quite simple," said Margaret in surprise. "We mustn't set ourselves up as judges of what's right and what's wrong. If people are sorry and show it we should forgive them—but not otherwise."

Walter digested this in silence. Margaret had put her piece of philosophy into very simple words but it went deep. He had not expected deep, clear thinking from this surprisingly charming little sister. He realised the truth of what she had said and saw the implications: he had behaved badly but he was sorry and was showing it so he would be forgiven. The words, 'but not otherwise' were stern words and sounded all the more stern coming from the gentle Margaret . . . but they also were true. Repentance had to come before forgiveness.

Margaret was looking very thoughtful and Walter wondered what was coming next. At last she said, "You'll stay to lunch, won't you? I was just wondering if there would be enough, but it will be all right. You'll stay, won't you, Walter?"

He could not help smiling. "Well, if you're sure it wouldn't be a bother—"

"No bother at all—and I promise there will be enough to eat. Bernard is coming home to lunch, so you'll see him," added Bernard's wife, offering the bait with confidence. Obviously she was of the opinion that no fish could resist it.

"Yes, I'd like to meet Bernard," said the fish.

3

Margaret had no domestic help (she liked being alone with Bernard, and the little house was so well-designed that she could manage it quite easily herself) so she was obliged to leave her guest to his own devices and betake herself to the kitchen. She gave him the daily paper and left him. For a time he scanned the news and then he put down the paper and looked about him—and meditated.

Why had he told Margaret all that? He certainly had not intended to . . . but somehow he had felt she would understand. As a matter of fact Walter was by no means the only person who had found himself telling Margaret more than he (or she) intended for Margaret was a good listener and deeply interested in her fellow creatures. But Margaret did not pour out sympathy to the undeserving. She had integrity, and sometimes people who expected sympathy were a little startled by the way in which she went straight to the point. Walter himself had been a little startled.

There were several photographs on the top of the bookcase—photographs of the family of course. Walter got up and looked at them with interest. This one obviously was Bernard. It was a rugged sort of face; not really good-looking, but with plenty of bone, plenty of character. It was a trifle stern but there was a latent twinkle in the deep-set eyes; it was the sort of face you would look at twice, Walter decided. And this must be his youngest half-sister, little Rose. She was very young and extremely pretty—as pretty as her name. And here was his stepmother; Walter remembered her of course and he thought he would have known her even if he had seen this photograph in some other place. Naturally she was older, he had known her as a young girl and this was a middle-aged woman, but her face had not really altered, it had only matured. She was like Margaret (or, more correctly, Margaret was like her). The expression was the same, gentle and kindly. He turned from her picture to the fourth and last; this must be Delia! Like the others she was dark-haired and good-looking but her expression was entirely different. Discontented, perhaps frustrated, thought Walter. Yes, Delia had a chip on her shoulder. He wondered why. The look of frustration did not put him off, in fact it interested him, for he himself had felt frustrated. He knew what it was to feel a grudge against the world. Hard gruelling work, disappointments, and at long last success had helped Walter to get rid of his chip. She needs to knock about a bit, decided Walter as he put back Delia's photograph and straightened it carefully.

4

Bernard came home to lunch, as Margaret had promised; she had promised that there would be 'enough to eat' and most certainly there was. It was an excellent meal, well cooked and nicely served without fuss or bother. Walter's opinion of his young hostess rose considerably. They drank a light Spanish Graves and chatted in a friendly manner.

When they had finished Margaret left the two men together and Walter repeated his history for Bernard's benefit—this time in greater detail; he also repeated his offer of financial aid.

"That's good of you," said Bernard. "It relieves my mind considerably. We're all right at the moment but the time may come when we shall be glad of your help. Highfold is running away with a good deal of Esther's income. I'm hoping to sell it soon but meantime it has to be maintained. There's some dry-rot—that's the trouble. We're keeping it in check but it's a beastly thing. You never know where it may break out again in an old house like that."

They went on talking, there were several matters to be discussed. Walter explained that he had not returned to England only to see his family. He had some business to transact as well. He had hired a Daimler for the duration of his visit and intended to call upon stockists in various parts of the country to hear their views about Hallsey's goods and induce them to increase their orders . . . Bristol, Birmingham, Liverpool, Glasgow were some of the towns on Walter's list. All this would take time, of course, but it would be time well-spent. As manager of the firm, Walter had prestige; he could speak with authority and deal with 'the bosses' on an equal footing.

Bernard listened with interest. Like Margaret he had started with a prejudice against Walter, but he could not help liking the man—and obviously he was keen on his job and knew it inside out which was a mark in his favour and gained Bernard's respect.

"I hope you'll spend a little time at Shepherdsford," said Bernard. "You'll want to see the family and get to know them a bit."

Walter nodded, "Yes, I must do that. I'll be here to-morrow and the next day, and I'll come back again for a few days before I fly home. I'm staying at The Owl, that old inn near the river. It's a bit old-fashioned but it seems quite comfortable and I like the people who run it. You can always get in touch with me there if you want me."

"When do you propose to go and see Esther?" asked Bernard. "I had better warn her that you're coming."

"Yes, please tell her. I could go there to tea to-morrow if that would suit her. Perhaps you could explain why I didn't write before, and tell her I'm sorry I was such a fool."

"I'll explain some of it," said Bernard cautiously. "It would be better if you told her the whole story yourself. I don't think you will find Esther difficult; she's a very gentle creature—like my Meg."

Walter hesitated and then he said, "It's a small point, but I notice you call her Esther."

"What else could I call her?" asked Bernard smiling. "She's a comparatively young woman so it would be ridiculous for me to call her 'mother'—and 'Mrs. Musgrave' sounds unfriendly. I admit the problem gave me some thought but I just took the plunge and called her Esther. She didn't seem to mind."

"I see," said Walter doubtfully. "It's different for me of course."

Bernard refused to be drawn.

CHAPTER SEVEN

1

BERNARD had promised to ring up The Bridle House and tell Esther of Walter's arrival home and of his intention to call. Bernard's word was as good as his bond. In this case it was better, for after due thought he decided that the telephone was unsuitable for the purpose, partly because it is difficult to conduct an intimate conversation on the telephone and partly because in a small place like Shepherdsford the telephone is not always strictly private. He explained this to Margaret and suggested that she should visit The Bridle House in person and smooth Walter's path. Needless to say Margaret agreed.

"Of course, Bunny," said Margaret. "That girl in the telephone exchange would listen to every word and it would be all round the village in half no time. I'll nip over to The Bridle House and tell Mummie."

At first Esther was horror-stricken at the news. Walter was actually here! Walter wanted to meet her! The mere idea was appalling. She had most unpleasant memories of Walter: he had behaved abominably; he had upset her beloved Charles and made him utterly miserable. How could she possibly meet him? What could she say? It was all very well for Meg to talk so glibly of forgiveness; Meg hadn't been born—nor thought of—when Walter came to Highfold Park. Meg hadn't the slightest idea how awful it had been.

"Oh I know," said Margaret. "It must have been simply frightful."

"You can't imagine how frightful it was. You can't understand what I feel about it."

"I do understand," declared Margaret earnestly. "I understand because of loving Bunny. I mean if someone hurt Bunny dreadfully it would be very difficult to forgive them."

"I really think I'd rather he didn't come," said Esther.

But Margaret was a good ambassador and drew such pathetic pictures of the feelings which had induced Walter's behaviour, of the privations he had endured and of his sincere repentance that Esther's heart was softened It was never very hard.

"I suppose if he's sorry . . ." said Esther reluctantly.

"He is—really," Margaret assured her. "He's sorry and ashamed and he wants to be friends."

"Oh dear!" said Esther. "I suppose I must. Yes, he had better come to tea."

2

The meeting with Walter was not as difficult as Esther had feared. He arrived a little before the appointed hour and Esther, who had decided to have tea in the garden in the shade of her favourite tree, was carrying out the tray.

"Let me do that!" exclaimed Walter and took it from her hands.

When he had placed the tray on the table Walter said, "You know why I've come. I want to say I'm sorry for causing so much trouble and distress. I want to be friends—if you'll let me. I could say a lot more but I expect you'd rather I didn't."

"Much rather," said Esther gravely. She also could have said a lot more but it was useless to dig up the past. If friendly relations between Walter and his father's family were to be established the only way was to leave the past deeply buried and to start afresh.

"Delia will be here any minute," said Esther. "Rose is out sketching; they both want to see you, but we needn't wait. Would you rather sit in the shade or in the sun?"

They arranged the chairs and sat down.

Esther's hand was not very steady as she poured out tea and offered her guest tomato sandwiches.

"This is a charming little garden," he said. "How pretty your flowers are!"

"They're suffering from the drought. I do what I can for the poor things. We aren't allowed to use the hose of course but we give them our bath-water."

They talked about the weather and the drought.

These were safe subjects.

Esther found it unexpectedly easy to talk to him for the simple reason that he was so absolutely different from the Walter she remembered, different in appearance and different in himself. She remembered a white-faced sulky boy and here was a middle-aged man with a lean, bony face, bronzed with African sunshine—a pleasant agreeable man anxious to be friendly and with plenty to say.

The fact was Esther could hardly believe it was the same person.

Margaret had said he was 'like Daddy' and obviously had intended this as a recommendation (Esther had not taken it as such. She dreaded a resemblance to Charles); but Esther could see no likeness except once or twice when he smiled. Then there was a vague fleeting resemblance; his eyes crinkled at the corners in the same well-remembered way.

By this time they were talking of Walter's plans—of all the places he intended to visit and of the business he hoped to do—and he explained that if all went well he hoped to return to Shepherdsford for a long week-end before leaving the country. He added that he had spoken to the proprietor of The Owl and had arranged provisionally to give a family luncheon-party at the Inn on the Sunday. He hoped they would all come.

"Yes, of course," said Esther. "That would be nice. Sunday is a day of toil for me. Flo—my daily—doesn't come on a Sunday so I have to get up early and prepare lunch before I go to Church. It's always delightful to go out to lunch on a Sunday . . . and it will be nice to see you again," she added with a charming smile.

When he saw the smile Walter knew he was really and truly forgiven. "That's good of you, Mrs. Musgrave!" he exclaimed.

"You had better call me Esther—if you feel like it," she told him. "Bernard does."

"That's *very* good of you, Esther," said Walter gravely.

3

When the girls returned things went even more easily. Rose was delighted with her stepbrother and chatted to him as if she had known him all her life; and even Delia, who had been extremely reluctant to meet Walter 'after the horrid way he had behaved', came out of her shell and told him about the Dramatic Club and how she had been chosen to play the leading lady in the forthcoming production.

Then Walter produced a small box of coloured slides and a projector and showed them pictures of the Hallsey estate, and pictures of his own bungalow with its wide veranda. There were several pictures of Walter himself and of his dog and a little group of native servants. It certainly was a beautiful place—a place of bright sunshine and wide horizons and gorgeously-coloured flowers.

They spent some time admiring Walter's slides and then Rose fetched the family album with photographs of Highfold Park and of the Musgrave girls in various stages of development. Esther had tried to prevent this from happening, saying she was sure Walter would be bored, but Walter was not in the least bored and looked at every picture most carefully.

It was Charles's album. Charles had taken the snapshots himself and pasted them into the book and had written amusing captions beneath each little picture . . . and when Esther saw Walter and Delia and Rose talking and laughing together over Charles's album she simply could not bear it. She had made up her mind to forgive Walter but this was going too far and too fast for her liking. She knew it was a 'wrong' feeling (for if you forgive you must forgive completely) and she knew it was unreasonable to be annoyed with Delia and Rose. Neither Delia nor Rose could understand what agony of mind Walter had caused their father—nobody who had not been there at the time could possibly understand.

Yes, it was wrong and unreasonable but all the same Esther wanted to seize the precious album out of their hands and take it away and hide it from them (it was quite insane but that was how she felt) and the desire to rescue the book was so intense that she could scarcely resist it. So she made an excuse and left them to it and went upstairs and battled with her feelings in the privacy of her own room.

CHAPTER EIGHT

1

THE Dramatic Club was delighted to enrol a new member, especially one who was reported to have done quite a bit of acting and could play accompaniments when required, so

Delia took Mrs. Winter to the first rehearsal of *The Mulberry Coach* and introduced her to everyone there. They were holding the rehearsal in Mrs. Blake's drawing-room as usual. The room was not very suitable for the purpose (it was far too small and cluttered up with furniture) but it was no use hiring a hall and paying money for it until the play had begun to take shape.

The play had been chosen and the characters cast so there was no part for the new member.

"What a waste!" exclaimed Helen Carruthers. "Couldn't we rearrange the cast—or choose another play!"

"For heaven's sake!" exclaimed Freddie Stafford in alarm. "Are we to go all over it again?"

"I thought you didn't like *The Mulberry Coach*," said Sylvia Newbigging.

"I don't," replied Freddie. "I told you why—we can't afford it—but we've chosen it now and we can't keep on chopping and changing every five minutes—"

"You mustn't *think* of it!" cried Eulalie Winter. "I shall be perfectly happy watching you, and I can do odd jobs and make myself useful."

"I still think it's a waste," murmured Helen . . . and several of the others agreed.

Obviously the new member was approved. Delia was delighted to see her protégée such a success.

While the rehearsal was in progress the new member sat upon a sofa which had been pushed into a corner of the room. She was not wearing slacks of course; she was wearing a black satin frock, very short and so tight-fitting that every curve of her figure could be seen. Her long legs appeared to advantage in sheer nylon stockings, and a necklace of amber, jet and crystal with dangling earrings to match completed the picture of elegance and charm.

Freddie Stafford sat down beside her. He sighed and said, "Did you ever see such a mess?"

"It seems a bit chaotic," admitted Mrs. Winter. "There's a lot of argument, isn't there? And none of them seem to know their lines. Why aren't you in it?"

"I'm supposed to be the producer. I'm also the director, the actor-manager, the scene-shifter, the publicity agent—and several other things as well."

"It sounds like a man-size job."

"Yes, doesn't it?" agreed Freddie. "I must have been mad to take it on—or possibly drunk. I've done the job several times for this blue-pencil club and every time I vow never to do it again."

"And then you do it," said Mrs. Winter smiling at him.

"Then I do it. As a matter of fact there's nobody else who could cope. I only wish there were."

"You seem to be rather scarce of men," suggested Mrs. Winter whose eyes had informed her of this deplorable fact.

"Yes. Too few men and far too many women. That's what's the matter with this club. I go touting round the district trying to persuade chaps to join, but most men hate dressing up and making fools of themselves so it's a bit hopeless."

"A pity I'm not a man."

"Definitely not a pity," declared Freddie looking at her sideways. He added, "Would it be impertinent at this stage of our acquaintance to ask where you got that delightful necklace? I've never seen one the least like it before."

"It *is* nice, isn't it?" she replied. "George bought it for me in Florence when we were on our honeymoon. George had very good taste."

"Obviously," declared Freddie with emphasis.

"I meant in choosing clothes."

"I didn't," said Freddie.

"You ought to be doing your job instead of sitting here wasting your time."

"But I'm not wasting my time."

She laughed.

"And anyhow," continued Freddie, "I can't start producing until some of them know their lines, and this room is singularly unsuitable for our purpose. It's like a junk shop. Have a heart, Mrs. Winter!"

"I was wondering," said Eulalie Winter thoughtfully. "I've got a music room at Fairways; it's quite a large room and there isn't much furniture in it so there would be more space to move about. Would it cause a lot of bother if I offered it to the club for rehearsals?"

"Edna Blake would take it as a personal insult."

"Then we can't—"

"Yes we can. I don't care a hoot what Edna Blake says."

"She might resign from the club—or something."

"No such luck," declared Freddie. "It would be good riddance of bad rubbish. We should get on much better without her and her tantrums. If you mean it seriously—about the room—I accept here and now."

"Come and see the room first."

"When can I come?"

"Any time you like. What about to-morrow?"

"It would have to be late—after dinner. I work during the day."

"On Sundays?" asked Eulalie, raising her eyebrows.

Freddie nodded. "Sunday is the busiest day of the week."

"You don't look like a parson."

"A parson? Oh, I see what you mean," said Freddie laughing. "No, that's not my line. Guess again."

"I can't think of anything—" she began.

"Freddie!" exclaimed Delia, appearing before them suddenly. "Freddie, what on earth are you doing? We're in a frightful mess."

"I can see that," he told her.

"Well, why don't you come and sort things out? You're supposed to be producing this play, aren't you?"

"Yes," agreed Freddie, lolling back on the sofa and crossing his legs. "I'm producing this play. I have my own method. At first I watch what everyone is doing—I'm watching very carefully—and I make notes of all the mistakes. Then, and not till then, I stand up and shout. If you don't like my method you can get someone else."

"You know perfectly well there's nobody else!"

"In that case you'll have to put up with me and my method, won't you?"

Delia hesitated. Her temper was rising. She was aware that Freddie was teasing her—but what could she do? Freddie was lazy and frivolous, but when he began to take an interest in the proceedings he was good at his job.

"I wish there was somebody else!" exclaimed Delia.

"You can't wish it more than I do," Freddie assured her. "Get a move on," he added, waving his hand languidly. "It's the scene at the Inn. You're eloping with Ralph. I can't think why you're eloping with Ralph—you must be crazy—but that's what it says in the book. It says," continued Freddie, producing his copy and turning over the pages rapidly, "it says, 'Enter Angela and Ralph, eloping.'"

"I know, but I don't quite see—I mean how are we—"

"You must get it across somehow. I suggest you should creep in furtively, hand-in-hand; gaze round the room like scared rabbits and embrace with ardour."

"I've got to go," said Mark Henderson, who was taking the part of Ralph. "Awfully sorry—and all that—but I promised I wouldn't be late."

"The night is young."

"I know, but Joan is waiting up for me."

"There goes a good man spoilt," said Freddie to Mrs. Winter. "You'd scarcely believe it but Mark was quite a bright lad before he entered the state of matrimony." Mark's departure had started the rot. Everyone was glancing at watches, saying good-bye and searching for coats and wraps.

"Is it over?" asked Mrs. Winter in surprise.

"It's over," replied Freddie. "Let's elope, shall we? Let's creep out furtively hand-in-hand while nobody is looking. I'll run you home in the car. Have you got a coat?"

Mrs. Winter had a white fur stole, which was lying beside her on the sofa, so there was no delay. Freddie seized it and put it round her shoulders and they crept out furtively by the side door.

2

Delia was one of the last to leave and was surprised when she discovered that her protégée had vanished. (I suppose she got sick of it, thought Delia, but she might have said good night). It was disappointing, because Delia had been looking forward to walking home with Eulalie Winter and talking about the rehearsal, telling her about the different members of the club, discussing their various peculiarities and giving her a little warning about Freddie. Delia had noticed that they were getting on very well together. Of course Freddie could be amusing when he liked, but he was a notorious flirt and the sooner Eulalie was warned about him the better.

Delia had begun to call her new friend Eulalie when speaking of her to others but, so far, not to her face. She felt a bit flat as she walked home alone. She had been pleased when she saw that her new friend was so popular and such a success, but now she was not quite so pleased; everyone seemed to have forgotten that it was she who had brought Eulalie to the rehearsal. Everyone including Eulalie herself.

3

Meanwhile the 'elopers' were sitting comfortably in the music room at Fairways, partaking of refreshments.

"Yes, it's a ghastly mess," Freddie was saying. "But it always is at first so I'm not worrying. You'll be surprised when you see it 'on the night'. It will be quite passable, believe me."

Eulalie did not believe him. She said, "Of course it's none of my business but I think the play is miscast."

"Oh, it is! Delia is hopeless as Angela, but it's her turn to play lead—that's how we do things in the Shepherdsford Dramatic Club! And she's so disagreeable if she thinks she isn't getting her rights! Mark wasn't too bad before he got married—"

"He's extremely bad now; not only bad but half-hearted into the bargain."

"Oh I know, I know! Don't rub it in. The fact is he's terrified of Delia . . . but who else is there? You saw the whole club assembled to-night. Who else can you suggest?"

"Why didn't you take the part yourself?"

"Now you're asking," declared Freddie. "The answer is, Delia doesn't attract me—see?" He paused for a moment and then added thoughtfully, "I wonder if I could get Edward."

"Edward who?"

"Edward Steyne. He's here just now, staying at Underwoods with his stepmother. I wonder if he would be any use."

"He couldn't be worse than Mark."

Freddie smiled somewhat ruefully. He said, "Listen, Eulalie, I believe that's the answer, I shall—"

"Who gave you permission to call me Eulalie?"

"I thought it was your name," said Freddie in mock surprise.

"Supposing I told you it wasn't?" she said, laughingly.

"I shouldn't believe you, that's all. You couldn't possibly be called anything else. It was very clever of your godfathers and godmothers to give you that name. They must have been inspired. I mean all babies look alike, don't they?"

"What nonsense you talk! Have another sandwich, Freddie."

"Thank you, Eulalie. I'll have two. I've earned them."

"Earned them!" she exclaimed, raising her eye-brows. "You've done nothing whatever to-night except sit on a sofa and talk to me. Was that very hard work?"

"Not very," he admitted, smiling.

"Talking of work, I've been trying to guess what you do for a living that keeps you so busy on Sundays. You aren't a parson."

"No."

"I can't think of anything else," declared Eulalie looking very thoughtful.

"Try hard," suggested Freddie. "You look terribly attractive when you're thinking."

"Do you ring the church bells?"

He shook his head. "Wrong again! That's two guesses. You've only got one more."

"You hand round the plate."

"Goodness no! Not me. They wouldn't trust me with the plate; I'm the bad boy of Shepherdsford. That's three guesses, so now you must pay the forfeit." He came round behind the sofa and took the forfeit very expertly.

"Supposing I had guessed right?" she asked, looking up at him and smiling.

"You would have received a prize of course. I'll show you the prize, shall I?"

He showed her the prize.

"You had better go now," said Eulalie. "It's getting late and to-morrow is your busy day."

Freddie agreed and went at once. He stopped at the door and looked back. "By the way," he said, "I'm Secretary of the Local Golf Club—that's all. Rather an anti-climax, I'm afraid."

As she tidied the room and plumped up the cushions Eulalie was smiling. She had decided that Shepherdsford would not be as dull as she had feared. A mild flirtation with Freddie would pass the time very agreeably.

CHAPTER NINE

1

SUNDAY was another gorgeous day, warm and sunny with clear blue skies. Esther awoke early and went downstairs to prepare breakfast. She sang as she worked for the fine weather made her happy . . . and Rose was here. Having Rose at home was even more delightful than Esther had expected—dear sweet little Rose, the baby of the family, and as such treasured and adored. No wonder Esther was happy this morning—any mother would have been happy. Of course Esther loved her other daughters every bit as much (one should not have favourites) but there was something extra special about Rose.

Like many other households The Bridle House was self-contained on Sundays (there was no outside help to be had) but Esther did not mind. She had a definite feeling that it was right. She could not have explained why, but it had something to do with the refugees—thousands of poor homeless creatures living in camps all over Europe without sufficient food or clothing! Of course one did what one could—one gave money and ran Jumble Sales—but that was not enough. Somehow Esther felt that in this modern world she ought to work with her hands; she ought to do things in the house; she ought to make beds and cook food for herself and her daughters to eat.

Before the war Esther, and others in her position, had done nothing in the way of household chores. Now it was different; people had to roll up their sleeves and do things for themselves. Life was more real, Esther thought . . . and if one organised the work of the house there was still time for reading and meditating; there was still time to 'stand and stare'.

On the whole people were happier, Esther decided. There were a few like Edna Blake who complained incessantly about the inconveniences of modern life and moaned aloud for the 'good old days' when one had 'real servants with caps and aprons'; but Edna Blake was a born moaner and would have found something to moan about if she had possessed a well-trained staff to wait upon her, hand and foot.

Compared with some of her friends Esther was lucky, for she had Flo Bloggs who came for a couple of hours every morning except Sundays. Flo was by no means 'a well-trained servant' but she scrubbed and cleaned and polished in a cheerful manner and brought all the news of

Shepherdsford to The Bridle House. Esther, who was in a frivolous mood this Sunday morning, tried to imagine Flo Bloggs in a cap and apron, but failed in the attempt. The mere idea was so ludicrous that she laughed aloud.

Esther liked Flo. There was something very nice about the girl. She was kind and willing and friendly. She was real all through. There was nothing underhand, nothing hidden in Flo's nature; Flo chatted in an artless manner about everything that came into her head. Esther had heard all sorts of things about the Bloggs family and their friends and their dog and their 'telly'. She had heard about the Dankses (who lived next door) and about Violet Danks and her boy friend, who was 'a traveller in jam' (a bit too smart, in Flo's opinion, but Vi was potty about him). All this was amusing—there was no harm in it at all—and there was no harm in Flo revealing the fact that Cynthia Cruft (who had been Flo's predecessor at The Bridle House) was now 'obliging' at Fairways every day from ten to two and 'that new lady, Mrs. Winter' had given Cynthia a lovely dress, almost new, which Cynthia had worn at the W.I. Party. And when Vi Danks left the Carrutherses' and went to the Blakes because they gave her sixpence an hour extra (well, there was no real harm in that) but when Flo added with relish, "Vi ses Mr. and Mrs. Blake 'ad words over the 'lectric bill and went on something awful," Esther received a very uncomfortable shock.

"You oughtn't to tell me things like that!" exclaimed Esther.

"Why ever not?" asked Flo in surprise.

Esther hesitated for it was difficult to explain.

"It's true, reelly," declared Flo. "Vi ses the Blakes 'ave 'orrible rows. They go it 'ammer and tongs. If it isn't the 'lectric bill it's something else. Vi ses—"

"That's the telephone!" cried Esther—and fled.

It was not Flo's fault of course. Flo simply did not understand what was permissible and what was not—and Esther could not explain. It isn't my fault either, thought Esther. How can I prevent the girl from chatting to me when we work together for hours every day? If I tried to shut her up she would think I was unkind . . . besides, I don't believe anyone could stop Flo flowing. Flo flows on for ever like the brook.

It was a horrible pun, but it made Esther laugh and she was laughing when Delia came into the kitchen.

"What are you laughing at?" asked Delia.

"It was rather silly," replied Esther, who had suddenly realised how silly it was. "I was thinking about Flo. First I tried to imagine Flo in a cap and apron, and then—"

"A cap and apron?"

"Yes, but I couldn't," said Esther giggling.

"Neither can I," agreed Delia. "But I can't see anything very funny about it. Why is it funny?"

"I don't know," admitted Esther. "It seemed funny to me—that's all. How did the rehearsal go off?"

"It was a complete fiasco. Freddie was in one of his silly moods."

"Did Mrs. Winter enjoy it?"

"She seemed to," said Delia shortly.

At that moment Rose came in and they all sat down to a modern frugal breakfast of cornflakes and fruit and coffee.

2

Esther had half promised Lady Steyne to call on Mrs. Winter but somewhat to her surprise she discovered that Delia was against it.

"You wouldn't like her," said Delia. "She isn't your sort of person at all."

"But I must do something about her. Perhaps we could ask her to tea."

"She doesn't like tea," said Delia.

Esther was silent. She had never met a woman who did not like tea.

The lovely summer weather continued unbroken and the Musgrave family, like many others, settled down to a hot-weather routine. They breakfasted earlier and got through the household work before lunch so that they could rest during the afternoon. Esther took a book into the garden and lay in a deck-chair beneath the trees and Rose lay on a rug beside her. Sometimes they read their books and sometimes Rose wrote long letters to her school friends but more often they talked. They had plenty to say to each other for Rose was like her mother in many ways. They had the same gaiety of heart, the same interest in their fellow creatures and they enjoyed the same sort of jokes. Rose had 'grown up' a lot in the last few months; there was more grace in her movements and her face, which had been chubby, had become more cleanly cut. Above all she had gained a dignity of manner which (her mother decided) was captivating in the extreme. But in spite of these signs of approaching maturity the real Rose was still very young indeed—young and innocent and guileless.

She's younger than the others were when they were seventeen, thought Esther. Is it because she's the baby of the family, or is it something in her nature which will never grow old? And is this childlike innocence a shield from the fury of wolves and the blandishments of serpents or is it a danger?

Esther could not answer her own questions.

3

Now that Rose had come home for good, Delia saw no reason why *she* should do anything in the way of household chores. Rose was no longer a child, she was supposed to be learning household management, so she might as well take over the few small duties which had been expected of Delia.

"Rose can wash up the breakfast dishes," she said to her mother. "She can help to make the beds and do the flowers, can't she? You see I've got to learn this part and it will take ages, so I shan't have time."

Esther agreed. Perhaps it was not very fair but Rose would not mind and it is much more pleasant to have a willing helper than a reluctant one.

The excuse offered by Delia that it would take her ages to learn the part, was unfortunately only too true. Angela babbled—there was no other word for it—and Delia was finding her babblings more and more tedious. She wrestled with Angela every morning, shut up in her bedroom, but she could not wrestle with Angela all day, so in the afternoon she usually went along to Fairways to see Eulalie Winter. The two had not very much in common, but all the same their friendship ripened quickly for Delia found Eulalie exciting and Eulalie found Delia useful.

There was still a great deal to do at Fairways and although Delia had been an unwilling worker at home she was delighted to help her new friend in any way she could. She polished furniture; she helped to hang curtains and pictures; sometimes she worked in the garden which had been neglected for years (if her mother could have seen her she would have been considerably surprised). But it was not all work; occasionally they took the afternoon off and went out together in Eulalie's little car. Here again Delia was useful for she knew the country well; she could play the part of cicerone to perfection. Quite soon Delia discovered that her new friend had no interest in Roman Villas nor any other buildings of antiquity, what she wanted was information about the large houses in the vicinity and the people who owned them.

"That's Underwoods," said Delia as they passed a high wall with an archway in it. "The house is Queen Anne and rather attractive."

Eulalie slowed down—she never drove fast—and they had a glimpse of the front door with the fan-light overhead and the windows on either side with small leaded panes. The garden was full of old-fashioned flowers which filled the air with fragrance.

"It belongs to Lady Steyne," continued Delia. "Mother knows her very well but she's quite old, and doesn't go about much."

"You mean she won't call on me," said Eulalie.

This was exactly what Delia had meant. She had discovered quite soon that her new friend was extremely clever (sometimes Eulalie's perspicacity was quite alarming); she had discovered that if there was anything she wanted to hide from her new friend the only way of hiding it was to remain completely dumb . . . and sometimes even that method did not work. Eulalie seemed able to read her thoughts. Fortunately there were plenty of other subjects to discuss which were perfectly safe. There was one subject which Delia felt bound to mention; it was her duty.

"Freddie is amusing, isn't he?" she said. "Quite a lot of people find him amusing—but of course you can't believe all he says."

"Can you believe all that anyone says?" asked Eulalie solemnly.

"No, of course not," said Delia. "I only meant he's apt to make friends with people and then suddenly cool off for no reason at all. He and Helen were frightfully thick for a time, and before that there were other girls—several of them. It's just Freddie's way."

It was difficult not to laugh at this ingenuous warning, but somehow Eulalie managed it . . . and she managed to reply with complete gravity that she would be on her guard against the wiles of Mr. Stafford.

CHAPTER TEN

1

ONE afternoon when Delia arrived at Fairways she found Eulalie lying in a hammock slung between two trees.

"It's too hot to do anything," explained Eulalie. "If you want a deck-chair there are several in the garage or you can get a rug out of the chest in the hall."

Delia fetched a rug and spread it on the grass.

"Tell me more about your travels," said Delia. "You've been to so many interesting places and you describe them so well."

"Lots of people travel."

"I know, but so often it sounds boring when they tell you about their experiences. They tell you about the wrong things. I want to travel but I don't suppose I shall ever get away from Shepherdsford. I'm stuck here for ever and ever," declared Delia bitterly. "Sometimes it makes me feel quite wild."

"You feel like that?" asked Eulalie in surprise. "I had no idea—"

"Oh, I don't talk about it! What's the good? I feel like a tiger in the Zoo pacing up and down from one set of iron bars to another. You wouldn't understand—"

"I understand very well indeed. I felt like that myself—as if I were a prisoner in a cell! I wanted to see the world, I wanted to meet interesting people—"

"Why couldn't you?"

"No money. You must have money to travel, or else—"

"Or else what?" asked Delia with interest.

"Or else stay at home of course."

Delia glanced at her. That was not what she was going to say . . . but she was gazing up at the tree above her head and obviously intended to say no more.

"But then your aunt died and left you some money, didn't she?" asked Delia, pursuing the subject in her usual way. "And then you were able to go about—you were free to go anywhere you liked and see all the places you had dreamed of. How wonderful it must have been!"

"Yes, it was."

"She must have been very fond of you?" suggested Delia.

"Yes," said Eulalie. She said it with an air of finality and Delia—who knew her moods fairly well by this time—knew that the subject was closed. It was annoying because Delia would have liked to hear a lot more and if it had been anybody else Delia would have continued to question and cross-question the witness, but she was too much in awe of Eulalie—so she was silent.

For a little while they were both silent and then Eulalie said, "You'll have to study your part."

"Study my part?"

"Yes, the others are almost word perfect. Honestly Delia, you'll have to get down to it. I'm warning you for your own good. Freddie is beginning to get a bit fed up—"

"Freddie is horrid!" cried Delia. "When he jumps on me I'm lost—even the bits I know go completely out of my head—and it's a frightful part to learn. I've tried and tried—I don't believe I shall *ever* be able to learn it! If only it rhymed! It's easier to learn something that rhymes."

Eulalie hid a smile—'if only it rhymed!'—but all the same she was sorry for Delia. She was aware that some people found it extremely difficult to learn prose by heart.

"Perhaps I could help you," she suggested.

"Oh Eulalie, if only you could! I'm nearly desperate about it . . . but wouldn't it be a bore?"

For a few moments Eulalie did not reply. It would be a bore—already she was half-regretting her impulsive offer—but although Delia was rather tiresome at times and had very little sense of humour she had been extremely useful . . . and it was pleasant to be idolised and admired. Eulalie had received quite a lot of admiration from men but to be idolised and admired by a woman was a new experience. There was another reason for her offer to help—more complicated and less laudable—Eulalie disliked Helen Carruthers. At first Helen had been friendly and pleasant to the new member of the Dramatic Club, but recently there had been a change in her manner (Eulalie knew the reason, of course, but all the same she was annoyed by Helen's rudeness) and if Delia was unable to learn the part of Angela the alternative was Helen. Everyone in the Club was aware of this and Helen was just waiting to grab it at the slightest opportunity.

"If only you could help me!" repeated Delia. "If you would hear me say my lines and prompt me when I go wrong. I know it would be a frightful bore but you're so kind—"

"Get the book," said Eulalie. "My copy is somewhere in the music room. We'll have a go at it now."

They worked at Angela for nearly an hour and made a little progress. Then Eulalie threw down the book.

"That's enough for to-day," she said with a sigh. "We'll do some more to-morrow."

"I don't know why I'm so stupid," said Delia humbly. "There must be something wrong with my brain. Of course it would be easier if it wasn't such nonsense. There's no *sense* in what she says."

"Nonsense isn't always difficult to memorise."

"Not if it rhymes—like Lewis Carroll."

"Even if it doesn't rhyme," declared Eulalie smiling quite openly this time. "For instance there's a piece of nonsense that my aunt used to say when I was a little girl and I've never forgotten it."

"Was that the aunt who left you her money?"

"Oh, did I say 'aunt'? I meant my grandmother. She used to read Maria Edgeworth—everyone read Maria Edgeworth in those days. This piece of nonsense was quoted by Maria in one of her books, but it was composed by Samuel Foote."

Delia had never heard of Samuel Foote so she was silent.

"You aren't the only person who has never heard of him," said Eulalie with her usual perspicacity. "Few people have. The sad thing is that he wrote quite a lot, but everything he wrote is completely forgotten except this piece of nonsense. I'll say it to you if you like."

Delia nodded. She was not fond of nonsense but she saw Eulalie was anxious to say it and probably it was not very long.

"'She went into the garden to cut a cabbage-leaf to make an apple-pie,'" said Eulalie dreamily. "'And at the same time a great She-Bear, coming up the street, pops its head into the shop. What, no soap? So he died and she, very imprudently, married the barber; and there were present the Pickninnies and the Toblillies and the Great Panjandrum himself with the little round button on top and they all fell to playing the game of Catch-as-Catch-Can until the gunpowder ran out of the heels of their boots.'"

"Is that all?" asked Delia in bewilderment.

"Yes, that's all," replied Eulalie laughing. "And don't ask me what it means, because it doesn't mean anything. That's the beauty of it."

2

All this time Christopher's bicycle—which was to be a birthday present from his parents—was standing in Eulalie's back-kitchen. It was a nuisance to Eulalie not only because it was in the way and blocked the door of a cupboard but also because every time she saw it she remembered that Christopher was coming to stay . . . and she was not looking forward to his visit with any pleasure.

"Why did you say you would have him?" asked Delia one day, when Eulalie had been moaning about the prospect of entertaining her nephew.

"Connie asked me to have him."

"I know, but why didn't you refuse?"

This was quite a natural question, for Delia was aware that her friend was not in the habit of putting herself out for anybody.

For a few moments Eulalie was silent and then she said, "Connie made me say yes."

Most people would have left it at that but Delia scented a mystery and continued to probe. "I don't see why you should have him," she declared. "It will be an awful nuisance, won't it? We shan't have any peace while he's here . . . and supposing he gets mumps?"

"Mumps? Why should he get mumps?"

"Oh, didn't you know? There's a lot of mumps in the village. Flo was telling us about it this morning. And the children just go about with it; they don't bother with quarantine at all. Of course if Christopher has had mumps it will be all right, you can't have it twice, but if he hasn't . . ."

"Mumps!" exclaimed Eulalie again, but in quite a different tone. "Oh Delia, I believe that's the answer!"

"The answer to what?"

"To my prayer, of course," said Eulalie beginning to laugh. "It's a horrible complaint, isn't it? So painful and unpleasant—and you can get all sorts of complications with it, can't you?"

"Oh, I don't know," said Delia doubtfully. "I had it at school and it wasn't really so bad."

"You were lucky," Eulalie told her. "Mumps is a very bad thing. It would never do to run the risk of poor little Christopher getting mumps. I'm so glad you told me about it Delia. I must write to Connie at once."

"Do you mean she won't let him come?"

"I'm afraid not," said Eulalie sadly. "It's terribly disappointing but I'm afraid dear little Christopher's visit will have to be postponed—or perhaps put off altogether." She sat down at the desk and seized her pen and a sheet of writing-paper. "Don't go, Delia," she added. "You can post this for me on your way home." Delia sat down and waited. The nearest pillar-box was not on her way home—and of course Eulalie knew this—but Delia never dreamed of making any objection. It was Eulalie's habit to assume that people would go out of their way to oblige her—and people usually did. But not always, thought Delia, as she watched Eulalie's ready pen flying over the paper. For instance, how on earth had Connie made her say yes?

CHAPTER ELEVEN

1

BY THIS time the Dramatic Club was holding the rehearsals of *The Mulberry Coach* in the music room at Fairways. There had been trouble about it—as Freddie had foretold—Edna Blake had almost resigned, but not quite, and soon even she was obliged to admit that the sparsely furnished music room was better for the purpose than her comfortable drawing-room.

Eulalie made an excellent hostess; she received her guests hospitably and did not fuss—not even when her furniture was shoved about and chairs were piled one on the top of another. Most of the time she sat in a corner with the book in her hand and played the part of prompter, which, as everyone knows, is not an easy part to play. Several changes had taken place since the first chaotic rehearsal and in Eulalie's opinion these were all to the good. Most of the actors knew their lines; even Delia was improving.

At first Eulalie had been slightly disappointed that there was no part for her, but now she was glad for she found it very interesting to be a looker-on and to see the play take shape. Freddie was clever; there was no doubt of that. He had ceased to be frivolous; indeed he had gone to the other extreme and drilled the cast unmercifully.

On this particular evening he was even more merciless than usual for there was now only a fortnight to go before the first night. The club had decided to give the play twice: firstly in the Village Hall in Shepherdsford and secondly in the Town Hall at Ernleigh. Freddie was doubtful about the wisdom of this innovation but he was over-ruled.

"All right," he said. "Have it your own way; but do, for goodness' sake, realise that the audience at Ernleigh will be much more critical. Shepherdsford knows us and makes allowances but Ernleigh will take us on our merits. We'll get the bird if you can't do better. D'you think anyone will pay good money to see a sloppy mess like this? Pull up your socks and put a little pep into it."

"I know my part," muttered Tom Blake, who objected to being hauled over the coals.

"It isn't you I'm worrying about; it's Delia."

"Me!" cried Delia. "I've got ten times more to say than anyone else, but all the same I'm nearly word-perfect!"

"Are you? That's interesting," Freddie told her. "I hadn't noticed."

"What on earth do you mean?"

"I only mean that nobody can hear a word you say."

"I'll speak louder on the night. I don't need to shout in this room."

"You don't need to shout anywhere," declared Freddie with an elaborate show of patience. "Nobody wants you to shout. We should like you to be audible, that's all. Try that scene again. I want your conversation with the old nurse. It's an idiotic conversation, I grant you, but unless the audience can hear what you're saying they won't have a clue to what it's all about . . . and, for the love of Mike, do try to remember not to turn your back to the auditorium."

Already they had done the scene twice and the others were bored. Helen was not only bored, she was angry (all the more so because she wanted the part of Angela and had been fobbed off with the silly old nurse). They stumbled through the conversation for the third time that evening.

"Give me patience!" cried Freddie. "You've missed out a whole chunk of dialogue."

"Helen gave me the wrong cue."

"I didn't!"

"Yes, you did. You said, 'You'll break your father's heart, Miss Angela,'—and that's my cue for bursting into tears!" cried Delia with blazing eyes.

"Pity you can't put some of that pep into your part," murmured Freddie.

The comment was made sotto voce, but it was not inaudible to the other members of the cast. Several of them giggled hysterically.

For a few moments Delia stood quite still, speechless with rage and fury.

"It's quite true," said Eulalie's quiet voice from the corner. "It was just a slip. People are apt to make little slips when they're tired. I think it's time everyone went home to bed—not that I want to get rid of you but you've done a lot to-night."

"All right. Pack it in," said Freddie.

2

"It's going to be quite good," said Eulalie as she and Freddie tidied up the music room after the others had gone. "The whole thing is taking shape. I never thought it would. It's amazing!"

"Yes, but it always is amazing," he replied. "Anyone seeing the thing at the beginning would think it utterly hopeless and then quite suddenly it comes to life. That's what makes it worth while doing."

"I can see that," she said nodding.

"Any comments?"

"Well—yes," Eulalie said. "As a matter of fact the duel is frightfully unconvincing. Of course it's a difficult thing to stage—and not very safe."

"I know, but what can we do?"

"Have the duel off-stage—shouts and yells and clashing of swords—and then Giles staggers in covered with blood and faints on the ground."

Freddie looked at her in surprise. "I say! You've got something there," he declared. "Why couldn't I have thought of that myself? "

"It's easier for an onlooker," she told him.

This was not the first time Eulalie had suggested an alteration in *The Mulberry Coach*—and her suggestions had all been good. It was Eulalie who had suggested that 'Giles'—the villain of the piece—should be given a little more limelight. They had managed to get a young man called Ernest Lake to play the part; he was painfully shy for he came from the other side of Ernleigh and knew none of the other members of the club and as they all knew each other extremely well it was something of an ordeal. At first the unfortunate youth stood in the corner of the room and blushed when anyone spoke to him and it was thought by everyone that he was 'A Mistake', but when the play began to get going young Lake forgot to be shy and became a dashing villain. He confided to Sylvia (who was a kind-hearted girl and had gone out of her way to be nice to him) that his greatest ambition in life was to play Shakespearean Villains in Stratford Memorial Theatre and he hoped that when his parents saw him as 'Giles' in *The Mulberry Coach* they would agree to his proposal to give up his post in Barclay's Bank in Ernleigh and embark upon a stage career. Somehow or other Sylvia felt this was unlikely but as she had never met his parents she could not be sure.

"Have you any more brilliant ideas?" asked Freddie.

"Not really," replied Eulalie. "But I do think you're a bit hard on Delia."

"Well—perhaps," Freddie said thoughtfully. "I'll admit she's improved a lot just lately and she seems to have taken the trouble to learn her lines, but the fact is that girl gets under my skin."

"I can see she irritates you."

"She's like a tick," declared Freddie. "Yes, that's the word for Delia. You see quite a lot of her, don't you? How can you bear it?"

"I like her," Eulalie told him. "There's something worthwhile about Delia. She's got a temper, Freddie, and if you don't stop baiting her she'll throw in her hand—"

"Not she!" exclaimed Freddie laughing. "She wants to play Angela; she'll swallow anything."

When the room had been tidied Freddie went into the kitchen and carried in the tray of refreshments—this had become the usual procedure when rehearsals were over—and the two sat down and chatted in the usual manner.

They chatted for quite a long time, for they enjoyed each other's company and had a great deal in common, and then Freddie went away and Eulalie went to bed. Hitherto Eulalie had always washed up the glasses and plates and left everything tidy but to-night she was tired and could not be bothered and Cynthia was coming in the morning. What was the sense of paying Cynthia and washing up the things herself?

CHAPTER TWELVE

1

MR. AND Mrs. Bloggs had come to Shepherdsford soon after they were married. They had been born and bred within the sound of Bow Bells and the sound of Bow Bells still echoed in their speech and echoed in the speech of their daughters. At first they did not like Shepherdsford much—they missed the excitements of the city—but quite soon they discovered there were excitements in village life; different of course, but equally entertaining. Their cottage (which Esther Musgrave had described as 'polished and shining') was one of a row of cottages with gardens in a turning off the main street. It was an old cottage with small windows, sloping floors and few modern amenities but the Bloggses were fond of it. Mr. and Mrs. Bloggs had bought it with their combined savings so it was their very own. Mr. Bloggs worked on the railway and Mrs. Bloggs took in washing so a good deal of money rolled in weekly and they considered themselves comfortably off.

Now that the girls were grown-up and had good jobs they were even more comfortably off than before and there was no real need for their mother to take in washing.

"Why don't you give it up, Mimer?" asked Mr. Bloggs every time he saw the rows of snow-white linen dancing merrily on the line; and Jemima invariably replied, "I'd miss it, 'Arry. That's the truth."

Most certainly she would have missed it, for she was a born worker and there was not nearly enough to do in the little cottage to keep her busy—and she took a pride in the rows of snow-white linen which annoyed Mr. Bloggs so much. What's more it was interesting: quite a lot of local news could be learned from the garments that came her way. For instance Mrs. Bloggs knew that Mrs. Mainwaring's daughter—'her that married Mr. Summers'—had come home to Melville Manor and was going to have a baby. She knew when Mr. Edward Steyne came to Underwoods to stay with his stepmother: his pyjamas made you blink. She knew when Miss Helen Carruthers gave up her job in London and came home to Wisdon Hall to look after her parents, who were getting old and frail. Lovely things, Miss Helen had! But of course she *would* have lovely things, seeing she had been a mannequin in a posh London shop.

It was all very interesting indeed, and it gave Mrs. Bloggs something to talk about when the girls came home to supper or when a neighbour dropped in.

The Bloggses were a happy family; they had few troubles; they were all very fond of each other and very fond of their dog. The dog was no ordinary dog; they had not bought him nor acquired him in an ordinary way. One evening when they were having supper the dog had walked in through the open doorway and lain down by the fire.

"Look at that, now!" Mrs. Bloggs exclaimed.

"What a cheek!" said Daphne giggling. Daphne was always ready to giggle; perhaps that was why she was fat.

Flo had thrown herself down on the hearthrug and was stroking the visitor's head. "Oh Mum, 'e's a darling!" cried Flo. "Let's keep 'im. I've always wanted a dog."

"We can't keep 'im," declared Mr. Bloggs. "That dog belongs to someone—stands to reason."

Certainly it was reasonable to suppose that the dog belonged to someone. It was a full-grown animal, plump and well-looking—quite definitely not a stray—but it had no collar to give a clue to its identity.

"Where 'ave you come from, doggie?" inquired Flo.

The visitor merely wagged his tail and licked her hand.

"You see!" exclaimed Flo rapturously. "It likes me. It wants to stay."

"Looks like it," Mr. Bloggs agreed. "All the same I'll 'ave to tell the police—and the sooner the better."

2

The police station in Shepherdsford was very small. Sergeant Rambridge was digging in his garden when Mr. Bloggs appeared. He abandoned his peaceful employment reluctantly, ushered Mr. Bloggs into the office and listened to his story.

"There ain't no notice of a lost dog," he said. "We'll 'ave to fill up a form saying 'ow you found 'im."

"We didn't find 'im. You might say 'e found us—like I sed."

Sergeant Rambridge was too busy filling up the form to split hairs.

"You found 'im in your garden," said Sergeant Rambridge.

"Not reelly," objected Mr. Bloggs. "The dog walked in when we was 'aving our suppers—"

"I know. You told me that already, but there isn't no room to write all that on the form—and 'e must 'ave been in your garden first—stands to reason."

"I s'pose so," said Mr. Bloggs doubtfully.

The fact was Mr. Bloggs had a wholesome respect for the Law—as represented by Sergeant Rambridge—and although the Law was not in uniform, but was wearing a collarless shirt and grey flannel trousers, baggy at the knees, Mr. Bloggs felt disinclined to argue with it.

"What is 'e?" asked Sergeant Rambridge, pausing pen in hand.

"I told you: 'e's a dog."

"There's all sorts of dogs," said Sergeant Rambridge patiently. "There's fox-terriers and pekes and poodles and blood 'ounds and Alsatians."

"'E ain't none of those."

"What is 'e then? I got to write it down."

"I dunno," said Mr. Bloggs, scratching his head. "'E's a bit like a pug—but pugs ain't got long tails—and 'e's a bit like a spaniel—but spaniels ain't got snub noses."

"Pug," said Sergeant Rambridge, writing it on the form. He added, "That's all, Mr. Bloggs. You'll be 'earing about it in due course."

"What?" asked Mr. Bloggs. "I mean what'll 'appen?"

"If 'e isn't claimed 'e'll be put down. That's what."

"But—but we'd like to keep 'im," said Mr. Bloggs hesitating at the door. "The girls 'as took a fancy to 'im—quite dotty about 'im, they are—and it seems as if the dog 'as took a fancy to us. Walked in, 'e did, as perky as you please and lay down by the fire."

"If the dog's not claimed you can keep 'im but if 'e's claimed you can't. That's the Law," declared Sergeant Rambridge.

There was nothing more to be said.

When Mr. Bloggs got home and looked at the dog critically he felt pretty certain that the designation upon the form was incorrect, but the form had been filled in—so he left it.

The dog had no name (or at any rate the Bloggses did not know it) and this was found to be inconvenient. You could not call 'Dog, dog, dog!' when it was time for his dinner—not that there was any need to summon him for his dinner. He was always ready for food.

"We'll call him Puggy," said Mrs. Bloggs. "That's 'is name on the form." She held out a piece of meat and called, "Puggy!" and he came immediately. "There, what did I tell you!" exclaimed Mrs. Bloggs in triumph. "Puggy is 'is name."

3

The next few days were anxious times for the Bloggses. Every time there was a knock upon the door they felt sure it was Puggy's rightful owner, come to take him away; but nobody claimed Puggy and soon the Bloggses ceased to worry and came to think of him as their very own. Occasionally they discussed the matter and wondered about his origin; he must have come from somewhere they supposed. Dogs could not materialise out of thin air and walk into your house, could they?

"P'raps 'e came from the moon," suggested Daphne.

"I wish 'e could tell us," said Flo.

Whether or not he had come from the moon Puggy had shown admirable judgment in his choice of a new home. No dog could have been better fed or more comfortably bedded or treated with more affection and respect.

Soon after the arrival of Puggy the Bloggses bought a 'telly'; (it was essential to have one, because all their neighbours had 'tellies') but none of them liked it much. The fact was they were all great talkers and they found it more interesting to exchange news of their daily doings and the gossip of Shepherdsford than to look at and listen to the daily doings of the outside world, and they soon discovered that it was more comfortable to sit and talk quietly than to shout and bellow at each other with the 'telly' turned on full blast. Of course they turned it on full blast when a neighbour dropped in to see them because that was the right thing to do, but neighbours often brought news—interesting news about other neighbours—which the Bloggses wanted to hear.

"I dunno why we got the danged thing," declared Mr. Bloggs one evening when the 'telly' had been particularly troublesome. "I couldn't scarcely 'ear a word Danks was saying. It's just a nuisance, that's what."

"I couldn't 'ear Mrs. Danks neither," said Mrs. Bloggs with a sigh.

"We can turn it off now they've gone," said Flo, suiting the action to the word.

Peace fell like balm upon the little parlour and conversation at normal pitch was resumed.

"They've got one at Underwoods now," said Daphne. "Lady Steyne was always saying as 'ow she'd never 'ave one in the 'ouse, but Mr. Edward got it for 'er birthday—so there it is. Lady Steyne doesn't bother with it much—nor Miss Penney neither—but Mr. Edward looks at it a lot. This very morning 'e called me in to the lib'ry to look at something special, but I just sed I 'adn't got no time. I sed, 'No thank you, Mr. Edward. I got my work.' So then 'e sed 'you're lucky.'"

"Whatever did 'e mean?" inquired Mrs. Bloggs in surprise.

"Meant 'e 'adn't got no work," replied Daphne. "Miss Penney ses 'e's looking for a job but it's my belief 'e'd run like a rabbit if 'e saw one."

"You've always got your knife into Mr. Edward," declared Flo. "I'm sorry for 'im. Miss Barbie didn't ought to 'ave given 'im the go-bye like she did—"

"That's what *you* say!" exclaimed Daphne. "You don't know nothing about it. Miss Barbie would never 'ave done the dirty—a nicer young lady never stepped. She'd sit down in the kitchen with 'er elbows on the table and drink 'er elevenses and chat as natural as you please, and she'd 'and over 'er cup and say, 'you tell my fortune, Daphne, there's nobody tells fortunes as good as you. . . .' and two loverly dresses she gave me, when she was ill and got so thin, two loverly dresses which I'm wearing one now. So you can say what you please, Miss Barbie never done the dirty on nobody."

Daphne paused and looked round defiantly but none of her family contradicted her.

"Must 'ave been 'im then," said Mr. Bloggs nodding. "Must 'ave been 'im as done the dirty."

"Must 'ave been 'im," Mrs. Bloggs agreed.

Having decided on irrefutable evidence that the blame for the broken engagement lay at Mr. Edward's door, the Bloggs family passed on to other subjects and Flo, who had been put down severely by her elder sister, decided it was about time for her to take an active part in the conversation.

"I'll tell you something," said Flo, giggling. "That Mrs. Winter is a wunner and no mistake. She 'ad a gentleman in to supper late at night—sangwidges and beer and things, Cynthia sed."

This piece of news interested the Bloggses profoundly as Flo had known it would. Of course there was no need to ask how Cynthia knew of the supper-party at Fairways—that was self-evident.

"Might 'ave been a lady," suggested Mrs. Bloggs after a moment's thought. "Might 'ave been your Miss Delia, she goes there a lot."

"It wasn't, then," declared Flo. "Cynthia sed there wasn't no lipstick on the bits of cigarettes in the ashtray, see?"

CHAPTER THIRTEEN

1

ROSE had decided to go for a walk this afternoon. Instead of lazing in the garden she would climb the hill behind the village to the Abbey Woods—so called because of the ruins of an ancient Abbey which had once belonged to the Black Friars. Rose was enjoying the warmth and the sunshine of this lovely summer. She could not remember a summer like this. She could remember warm days, of course, but this long spell of warmth was different. Something inside Rose expanded and opened like a sunflower. She could wear light clothes—light as air—and she felt a sense of freedom as if her body were more her own. The golden sunshine blessed her skin.

When she came to the little gate at the bottom of the garden she leant against the wall and she could feel the heat of the wall through her cotton frock so that it seemed as if the very stones were friendly. There was a warm sweet scent of flowers in the air and the quiet lazy sounds of the golden afternoon drifted to her ears.

The path leading up to the Abbey Woods was steep and stony; the sun blazed overhead in a cloudless sky, but Rose did not mind the rough path, she went up it like a bird. She did not mind the heat, she gloried in it . . . then suddenly the path she had been following plunged into the woods.

Here beneath the shade of the trees it was cold and damp and dark. The change was so surprising that Rose hesitated—almost she turned and went back—and then her eyes became used to the gloom and she realised that it was not really dark for the sunshine penetrated the foliage of the old gnarled oaks and fell in golden patches on the ground. It was not really cold either, it was just cooler than it had been in the sunshine. She had made up her mind to visit the ruins of the Abbey so it would be silly to turn back.

The path was even steeper here, winding amongst the trees. In some places a tree had fallen and the path made a little detour to avoid the obstruction. Here and there she saw masses of nettles and willow-herb . . . there were brambles as well. Later she would come up here and gather baskets of blackberries to make delicious jelly. She must remember about that.

Rose had not been here since she was a child. She and Margaret had brought their tea occasionally and had picnics . . . but in those days Rose had not liked these woods, they had awed and frightened her. She had felt that at any moment she might see a Black Friar. Somebody must have told her about the Black Friars who had lived in the Abbey, but she could not remember who had told her. Once or twice she had mentioned her fear to Meg but Meg was so much older than herself and so much more sensible that she had not really understood. Of course when Meg laughed at the idea of a Black Friar wandering unhappily amongst the ruins of his home Rose had said no more about it . . . but the feeling of awe remained.

In those days Rose had been under the impression that a 'Black Friar' was a negro and this made him even more to be dreaded, for having read Prester John she had a vivid picture in her mind's eye of that strange terrifying creature practising black magic on the sea-shore and chasing the boys who had witnessed his performance; chasing them up the cliffs and almost catching them. It had given the young Rose nightmares for weeks. It was the word 'black' that made it all hang together—Black Friar, black magic, black Prester John.

How silly I was! thought Rose. I was a silly ignorant child. Now that I'm grown-up I'm not a bit frightened.

2

Presently Rose came to the glade where the ruins lay. It was a large shallow basin in the middle of the woods. The great oak trees surrounded the glade like sentinels. The sunshine poured down filling it with warm golden light; poured down upon the thick ruined walls and pillars and heaps of huge broken stones. It was very warm here and very quiet, there was not a sound—not even the twitter of a bird. Rose sat down upon a sun-warmed stone and looked about her; the broken walls and pillars and archways, the huge stones scattered upon the ground gave her a feeling of wonder. What sort of people had built this enormous place and how had it been destroyed?

For a time Rose sat there enjoying the warmth of the sun and thinking; first she thought about the Black Friars and then she thought about herself. In a way she was sorry that she was not going back to school, for she had enjoyed her years at St. Elizabeth's and had made some very good friends, but in another way she was glad. She would miss the games of course but lessons were rather a bore and most of her special friends were leaving—some to go to college, others to find jobs. Rose was the only one of her little coterie whose future was undetermined.

("You'll be bored stiff," they told her. "Nobody goes home and does nothing nowadays." "There's lots to do at home and Mummie needs me," Rose had replied.)

Rose was still musing in a sort of day-dream when a slight sound disturbed her. She looked up quickly, half-expecting to see a Black Friar, but all she saw was a tall young man, wearing pale grey slacks and a pale-blue shirt. Although he was not a Black Friar it gave Rose a little shock to see him—standing upon a pile of stones which had once been part of the chapel wall. He was high above her, his figure outlined against the sky and she could not imagine how he had got there. A few moments before he had not been there—and now he was. He had not seen her, that was obvious, for he was gazing over the tree-tops with field-glasses clamped to his eyes. This being so Rose was able to gaze at him to her heart's content.

But the concentrated gaze of a fellow-creature is apt to produce an uncomfortable feeling—especially when one believes oneself to be alone in a deserted place—and after a few moments the young man left off looking at the view and looked down instead. He looked straight at Rose and, seeing her, took off his hat and waved. It would have been silly to take no notice of this friendly greeting, so Rose waved back. The young man disappeared at once, as if by magic, and in an incredibly short space of time he was standing beside her on the smooth green sward.

During the interval Rose had time to wonder whether he had been an apparition—not a Black Friar of course—but when he reappeared it was obvious that he was made of flesh and blood, and that the reason he had disappeared so suddenly was not due to any kind of magic but merely because he had come down from the wall some other way. She saw now that he was not as tall as she had thought (looking up at him had made him seem taller) but he was slender and good-looking and he had a friendly smile.

"It was nice of you to wave," he said.

"It seemed silly not to. I mean I don't know you, so I suppose I shouldn't have waved, but—but it seemed silly not to," explained Rose.

"It would have been unkind—which is much worse."

"I suppose it is," said Rose doubtfully.

"Much worse. And not knowing each other can be easily remedied. Let's pretend the Black Friar has introduced us."

"Is he real?" asked Rose. "I mean is he a real ghost?"

"Quite real," replied the young man gravely. "Lots of people have seen him wandering amongst the ruins. I can't say I've actually seen him myself but that doesn't mean he isn't real, it only means I haven't the right sort of eyes."

It was natural that Rose should look at his eyes; they were large and brown and were looking at her with obvious pleasure. She looked away hastily. She was a little bit worried now for she was aware that it was 'Not the Right Thing' to talk to a strange man in a deserted place but she did not know how to break off the conversation gracefully.

"I must go home to tea," she said rising quickly.

"Please stay a bit longer," he said. "If you don't believe in the Black Friar we can introduce ourselves. I'm Edward Steyne."

"Oh, Mummie knows Lady Steyne!" cried Rose in relief. "I know her too—though I haven't seen her for ages. I'm Rose Musgrave. We used to live at Highfold Park."

"Well, of course! I might have guessed! I've seen your mother often and I've heard quite a lot about you and your sister. She married Bernard Warren, didn't she? My stepmother went to the wedding. So everything is all right. You can sit down and talk to me."

Rose hesitated. "All the same I shouldn't have waved."

"You should have—honestly. It would have been unkind not to. I expect you guessed I was unhappy. That was why you waved."

It had not occurred to Rose that he was unhappy.

"Terribly unhappy," declared Edward. "You see I was engaged to a girl, and we were going to be married, and then quite suddenly she changed her mind and married somebody else."

"How dreadful!" Rose exclaimed.

"Yes," said Edward, sitting down on the grass and putting his hands round his knees. "Yes, it was dreadful. We were so happy, you see, and then this other chap came along—and that was that. I suppose I'm not the only fellow that this has happened to. I suppose I'll get over it in time."

"Of course you will—and she can't be very nice to—to do that."

"I loved her."

"Yes of course, but honestly she can't be—very nice."

"It's some time since it happened. They're married now. As a matter of fact I was beginning to get over it a little and then I came back here to Underwoods and I'm miserable again. It was here, in this very spot, that I asked her to marry me—and she said yes."

"You shouldn't have come back!" exclaimed Rose. Edward did not answer and for a little while there was silence. Rose had sat down again upon the stone. She had forgotten that she had said she must go home to tea. At first Rose had thought that her new friend was quite young, a mere boy not much older than herself, but now she realised he was a good deal older. This gave her a feeling of importance. It was wonderful that a grown-up man should want to talk to her and tell her his troubles.

"You're so sympathetic," said Edward at last. "Nobody else seems to understand what I've been through. Even Amie doesn't care."

"Amie?"

"That's what I call my stepmother," Edward explained. "She used to be very kind and understanding, hut she's getting old. When people get old they don't understand things the same. You understand, don't you?"

"Yes of course. I just wish I could help."

"But you *are* helping! It helps tremendously just to sit here and talk to you. There's nobody else I can talk to like this." He paused and looked round and added in a low voice, "I keep on thinking about her."

"You must try to forget her."

"I suppose I must, but it's difficult."

"Yes, of course it will be terribly difficult—but you must try."

Edward looked up and saw that her eyes were soft with sympathy. He leant over and patted her knee.

"I've made you unhappy," he said. "It's frightfully selfish of me to bother you with my troubles, but you've made me feel better already. I was so lonely, you see." It occurred to Rose that her new friend might like to be entertained so she suggested he should come to lunch at The Bridle House. "Mummie would love to have you," she told him. "Mummie knows Lady Steyne, so it would be quite all right. We could fix a day—"

"It's terribly kind of you to think of it—but I couldn't," he replied, shaking his head. "Perhaps later on when I feel a bit better—but just at present I can't face a whole lot of people. You understand, don't you?"

"Yes, of course," said Rose. She realised she had said the same words several times already, but what else was there to say?

"If you could just meet me here sometimes," he continued. "We could talk a bit couldn't we? We could talk about other things—not just about me. But perhaps you're too busy?"

"I'm not busy at all except in the mornings, helping Mummie," Rose declared. She had almost said she had left school, but had stopped herself in time for he might think her terribly young and green. He had spoken to her as if she were properly grown-up. She was, of course (when you leave school you're properly grown-up) but all the same nobody had ever spoken to her like this before.

"Tell me about *you*," said Edward, smiling at her.

"About me? Oh, I'm not very interesting."

"I think you are. I think you're very interesting indeed."

Rose hesitated. She wished she could think of something to tell him—confidences to exchange for his—but she could think of nothing. Her prowess on the hockey-field would not interest him, nor the fact that she had taken the part of Rosalind in the school play.

Fortunately Edward did not wait for a reply. "I don't know what to do," he said sadly. "Perhaps you could advise me. You see I had a job in the City, but it wasn't the right sort of job—I was a square peg in a round hole—so I gave it up. You can't think how dull it was, sitting in an office all day. I stood it for a whole year, just to please Amie, but I couldn't stand it any longer. I've been offered a very good job in Kenya, growing tobacco, but Amie is old and frail and she hasn't anybody belonging to her except me."

"She would hate you to go so far away!"

"That's just the trouble."

"You mustn't go," said Rose firmly. "It would be very unkind to leave her like that; it might make her quite ill."

"You really think so?"

"Yes, honestly. You must get a job near her, so that you can go and see her—often."

"I expect you're right," said Edward reluctantly. "I don't quite know what I could do but perhaps something will turn up."

Rose had a feeling that these words were familiar (and oddly enough they gave her a slightly unpleasant sensation) however there was no time to think about that. She assured Edward Steyne that something was sure to turn up.

"I'd like to be a farmer," continued Edward dreamily. "It would be a grand life: getting up early and going to look at the cows being milked; having one's own land and growing things; being out all day long in the fresh air and the sunshine!"

"It wouldn't be so nice when it rained."

"Oh, I wouldn't mind a little rain."

Rose was not very enthusiastic about the idea for even to her inexperienced eyes her new friend did not look like a farmer. Farmers were big and tough—or so Rose imagined—and farmers did not wear pale grey slacks, beautifully creased, nor pale blue silk shirts.

They discussed other jobs which might suit Edward without getting much further . . . and then Rose glanced at her watch and gave a cry of dismay. "It can't possibly be half past six! Goodness, I shall have to fly!"

"Must you really?"

"Yes, really. Mummie will think I'm lost!"

"But we haven't decided—look here, you'll come back to-morrow, won't you? I mean it's important."

"Yes," agreed Rose, impatient to be gone. "Yes, of course—if you really think I'm any use—"

Rose fled home and arrived breathless. It was seven o'clock by this time and Esther had become really anxious about her—one read such horrible things in the papers—but obviously Rose had had no horrible adventures. Indeed she seemed on top of the world.

Rose intended to tell her mother all about Edward Steyne but she couldn't because Delia came in—she certainly was not going to tell Delia about her adventure—and Margaret and Bernard were coming to supper so there was no time.

"Run upstairs and change quickly," said Esther. "And you had better have a bath. You look frightfully hot."

Naturally she was hot. She had run all the way home.

CHAPTER FOURTEEN

1

ESTHER did not really enjoy having all her family together; she had to steer the conversation carefully which was rather a strain. It really was much more pleasant to have them separately. To-night, however, supper went off quite well; Delia was unusually talkative, Margaret was unusually silent and Rose seemed lost in dreams. It was not until they had finished supper and were sitting in the garden that trouble began to brew.

Esther did not know how it started for she had gone to make the coffee but when she came out with the tray she realised that the atmosphere had changed.

It was Delia of course. Delia was talking about Highfold Park and comparing its amenities with the discomforts of The Bridle House.

"We could have been sitting there now, on the terrace," Delia was saying. "So much more comfortable than this silly little garden. There's such a lovely view from the terrace. It was quite ridiculous to move. All we needed to have done was to draw in our horns a bit; to shut up some of the rooms—"

"But Delia, it was costing so much!" exclaimed Esther. "It was so cold in winter without fires in all the rooms and we couldn't afford to keep up the garden."

"I think your mother was right to move," said Bernard.

"You would! You advised her to move!"

"We both thought she would be happier," declared Margaret.

"She *is* happier—and so am I!" cried Rose. "This is a dear little house and so easy to run. We're ever so much more comfortable here."

"Don't let's talk about it," suggested Esther.

Delia turned on her. "It's all very well to say that, but you don't seem to realise that Highfold will soon be a ruin. You ought to go and look at it if you don't believe me. Eulalie and I walked over on Sunday—"

"But Delia we haven't enough money to keep it up properly."

"That's nonsense!" Delia cried. "That's penny wise and pound foolish. Eulalie says the place should be kept in proper repair if we want to sell it. Who's going to buy a ruin? The whole place needs to be painted; there are slates falling off the roof and some of the windows are broken—and I suppose you know that they're chopping down trees in the park! I never saw such a mess. It made me miserable to look at it—"

"Don't look at it then!" cried Rose. "There's no need to go and look at it."

"I'm not an ostrich, hiding my head in the sand!"

2

So far Margaret had taken no part in the discussion. She hated 'scenes' and she knew that her mother felt the same and would rather be trampled on than retaliate, but Bernard was different. Bernard had a temper. He had never been angry with her—not once in all the three years they had been married—but she had seen him get angry with other people. Bernard's temper was rarely roused; it was like a sleepy tiger, or perhaps more like a sleepy polar bear—a cold sort of creature. Margaret could see signs of the polar bear's awakening and she was alarmed.

"Bunny!" she exclaimed. "Bunny, let's go home!"

"Presently," said Bernard. "I just want to make things quite clear to Delia. She seems to have a wrong idea of your mother's financial position."

"A wrong idea! I've got no idea at all. Nobody tells me anything. You and Mummie keep everyone else in the dark."

"Oh, shut up, Delia!" cried Rose impatiently.

"You keep out of it," exclaimed Delia, turning upon her in wrath. "Children should be seen and not heard."

"I wasn't a child when you wanted me to make the beds and help Mummie in the house! Was I?" retorted Rose.

"I am perfectly willing to tell you anything you want to know," declared Bernard taking no notice of the interruption.

"I merely want to know why Highfold is being allowed to go to rack and ruin."

"It is *not* going to rack and ruin. The roof is being repaired, the outside paint-work has been attended to—perhaps you didn't notice that when you were there on Sunday afternoon. I was aware that the pantry window was cracked and I've had the pane replaced."

"And I suppose it was you who gave orders for the trees in the park to be torn up by the roots! The beautiful trees that Daddy was so fond of! I never saw such a mess. Eulalie said—"

"Delia, listen!" cried Esther in alarm. "The trees were—"

"It was I," replied Bernard, raising his voice and talking them both down. "It was I who gave orders for the trees to be felled and their roots removed from the ground. The trees are ripe for felling. I had my doubts about those trees and succeeded in getting an expert in forestry to come and look at them. He confirmed my suspicions. The trees had actually begun to deteriorate but fortunately not seriously. We sold the timber for a good price which will help to pay for repairs to the house."

"Bernard has been very clever about it," put in Esther.

"Why weren't we told?"

"You didn't seem interested," said Bernard. "If you're interested in the various plans for the maintenance of High-fold you can come to my office and I'll show you the accounts and balance sheets. I can assure you they are in good order.

"I don't want to see them!"

"You will come to my office to-morrow morning, Delia. I insist upon it. You've made allegations against me which I refuse to overlook."

"I'm too busy," said Delia sulkily.

"Busy! You're busy amusing yourself and dancing attendance upon Mrs. Winter!"

"Dancing attendance! How dare you, Bernard!"

"That's what I said. It would be a great deal better if you found a job and earned some money; better for yourself and better for your family."

"How can I?" cried Delia. "What could I do?"

"You're a perfectly healthy young woman. Why should you be unemployable?"

"It's all right," began Esther breathlessly. "There's enough money. Delia has never been very strong—"

"Strong enough to play golf all morning and stay up half the night rehearsing a play! Strong enough to—"

"But that's different!" cried Delia. "Eulalie says—"

"Eulalie!" exclaimed Bernard with a scornful laugh. "Eulalie says this and Eulalie says that! Can't you see what a fool you're making of yourself, Delia! Ask her why she calls herself by that ridiculous name."

"Oh Bunny, don't!" cried Margaret in dismay. "Bunny, please—please don't tell her!"

"Don't tell me what?" demanded Delia. "I don't know what you mean."

"I mean exactly what I say," declared Bernard. "Ask your friend why she calls herself by that ridiculous name. Ask her and see what she says. The last time I saw her she was called Aggie. It's some time ago and she's changed a good deal—"

"You must be mad!"

"Ask her if you don't believe me. We were fellow passengers on a trip to New York in a ship named the Cassandra."

"It must have been somebody else!"

"It was the same woman. In those days she was a down-trodden creature with prominent teeth and sandy hair—not at all attractive. She was companion to a rich old lady called Mrs. Frome—not a very pleasant old lady. Poor Aggie, what a time she had! Aggie had to fetch rugs and cushions, Aggie had to read aloud. She had to give up her seat if the old lady wanted to chat with one of the other passengers—and make herself scarce. At first I was sorry for the wretched Aggie but I needn't have wasted my sympathy. It was all done for a purpose; Aggie was no fool."

There was a short but very uncomfortable silence. Then Esther said, in a breathless voice, "But Bernard, are you sure? And—and anyhow it's not illegal to—to change your name."

"Dear me, no," agreed Bernard. "I never said it was. Anyone can change her Christian name and dye her hair. And there's no law against toadying to a silly old woman and inveigling her into altering her Will. Sometimes the old woman's relatives make trouble—that's the only danger."

"I don't believe a word of it!" Delia cried.

"Believe it or not," said Bernard. "It doesn't matter to me one way or the other. As a matter of fact she has changed so much that at first I didn't know her. It was only when I saw the amber necklace that I was sure."

"The amber necklace!"

"Yes. Amber, crystal and jet—a most unusual necklace. Mrs. Winter was wearing it the other night when we met her at the Newbiggings' dinner-party. That necklace belonged to Mrs. Frome—"

Delia interrupted him. "You're wrong there anyhow!" she cried. "Eulalie's husband bought it for her in Florence when they were on their honeymoon."

"I doubt it," said Bernard. "I'm inclined to think Mrs. Frome left it to Aggie in her Will—and a good deal more besides." He rose and added, "Come on, Meg. We had better go home."

Margaret rose at once. She was not so stricken as the others for she had known all this before. First she had been told of Bunny's suspicion—that Eulalie was Aggie in disguise—and then she had been told about the necklace. She had been let into the secret on the ground floor. The strange thing was it had seemed rather comical—she and Bunny had thought it rather a joke—but now it did not seem funny at all.

Margaret felt as if she had been run over, flattened out by a steam-roller. All she wanted was to go home—to her own peaceful home. She was so upset that she scarcely waited to say good-bye but hastened out to the car as fast as her legs would carry her.

"Bunny, you shouldn't have!" she exclaimed as she got in.

"It's my damnable temper; I can't help it; Delia gets my goat every time."

"Oh Bunny, it was dreadful."

"I know. I'm sorry, Meg. Your mother is an angel to stand the way Delia behaves."

"Yes, Mummie is an angel."

"Rose has begun to rebel. Did you hear her tell Delia to shut up?" He chuckled and added, "There will be fireworks in the family before very long. Mark my words!"

Margaret thought there had been fireworks to-night but she was too wise to say so. It was better to change the subject.

"Rose seemed—quite different—to-night. Not like herself, somehow."

"She's growing up, that's all."

"I wonder if that's all," said Margaret thoughtfully.

3

Margaret was not the only member of the family to be upset by the 'fireworks' and to feel as if she had been run over by a steam-roller. Esther felt exactly the same . . . and after her other daughters had gone to bed she sat by the open window in her bedroom and looked out on to the garden—and thought about all that had happened.

She was not worrying about Eulalie Winter, whether or not Bernard was right did not concern Esther in the least (Esther scarcely knew the woman, she had met her once or twice in Delia's company but that was all). Esther was worrying about her daughters, for they were definitely her concern.

How strange it was to have three daughters, all completely different! They had all been brought up in the same way with the same background, and in outward appearance they were not unlike, but inwardly there was no resemblance at all: Delia so prickly and difficult; Meg so sweet-natured and sensible; Rose so gay and happy and young!

It had been a worrying day for Esther; one of those days when everything seems to go wrong. She had worried desperately when Rose was so late in coming home . . . and then Rose had arrived hot and breathless, but looking extraordinarily pretty. At the time Esther had not thought much about it—she was busy preparing supper—and her only feeling had been one of relief to see the child arrive home in safety. But now she began to wonder what Rose had been doing (She was going to tell me something, thought Esther, I'm sure she was. If Delia hadn't come in at that moment . . . but it couldn't have been anything very important).

Then there was Delia. For the last fortnight Delia had been even more difficult than usual, and of course it was perfectly true that she was making a fool of herself over Eulalie Winter, which was unfortunate to say the least of it. If the woman were really an adventuress (which Bernard's story seemed to imply) it was more unfortunate still. To-night poor Delia had been terribly upset over Bernard's revelation and had rushed away madly the moment the Warrens had gone. If it had been one of her other daughters in distress Esther would have followed and offered comfort, but she was aware that she could not comfort Delia. When Delia was in distress she preferred to be alone. Esther wondered rather miserably whether Delia had gone to sleep by this time, or whether she was lying awake suffering in silence.

Then there was Meg, thought Esther. As a rule Esther did not worry about Meg; there was no need to worry about Meg for she sailed through life without any trouble; but just lately it had seemed to Esther that Meg was not quite so happy as usual. At times she was gay and merry, as if she hadn't a care in the world, but once or twice when Meg was sitting quietly, Esther had noticed a look of sadness on her face . . . and why on earth Meg should be sad when she had a devoted husband and a charming little house Esther could not imagine. There was another thing—a small incident which Esther had scarcely noticed at the time but which had returned to her mind later—she and Bernard had been sitting on the seat in the front garden and she had been trying to thank him for all he had done; she had told him he had "made Meg happy" and he had replied, "I've tried to". He had said it in an odd sort of way, as if he had intended to say more, and then he had changed the subject abruptly and had started to talk about business matters. Then Meg had arrived and there had been all that fun and nonsense about Mrs. Winter. . . .

It was not much, thought Esther. It was nothing, really; just a straw in the wind! But a straw in the wind shows which way the wind is blowing and once she had thought of the little incident she could not get it out of her head. She could not ask, of course. She could not say to Meg, are you happy? She could not mention the matter to Bernard. She would just have to wait patiently until she was told—or not told.

Oh goodness, thought Esther, what a fool I am! Why can't I sit back and leave things to take their course—as Charles always said?

It was at times like these that she missed Charles so dreadfully. His outlook had been so broad, his judgment so sure, his advice so wise. If Charles had been here she would not have had to carry the burden of their somewhat troublesome family alone; they would have talked it over together and she would have felt comforted.

4

Esther had been sitting at the window for a long time—how long she did not know—when she heard someone walking on the gravel path. She looked out and saw that the midnight prowler was Delia.

"Delia! I thought you were in bed!" cried Esther.

"Oh, you're awake! That's lucky. I was wondering how to get in. The doors are all locked. I'm sorry, Mummie, but you'll have to come down."

"Just a minute!" cried Esther.

As she hurried downstairs Esther found herself bewildered and surprised; not so much because Delia was out (though that in itself was sufficiently surprising) but because Delia's voice had sounded so cheerful. Esther had imagined her lying in bed, suffering torments, and, instead, she had gone for a walk . . . and, instead of being annoyed when she discovered herself locked out, she had actually apologised for the trouble she was giving.

Esther unlocked the garden door and let Delia in.

"I'm terribly sorry," said Esther, "I had no idea—I mean of course I thought you were in bed. It never occurred to me—"

"I went to see Eulalie," said Delia with a slightly defiant air. "I suppose you think it was silly but I just couldn't wait until the morning. I was so upset."

"Of course you were upset!"

"You see, Eulalie is my friend."

"Yes, I know—"

"Eulalie is my friend," repeated Delia. "So I had to see her at once and tell her about it. If people said horrid things about me behind my back I'd much rather my friends told me and gave me a chance to explain instead of brooding over it and getting all worked up."

Esther agreed with this. Most certainly it was the right thing to do, but all the same she did not think she could have done it herself. It would have taken more courage than she possessed.

"So that's why I went," Delia added.

"It was very late—"

"Yes, but I knew she wouldn't have gone to bed. She sits up till all hours."

"You—asked her?"

"I just said did she know anyone called Aggie, and she laughed and said, 'Oh, poor Aggie. How did you hear about Aggie? She's a cousin of mine. Some people think she's a little like me but I can't say I'm flattered.'"

"Oh Delia, what a good thing you asked her!"

"Yes, isn't it? The whole thing was cleared up in a minute."

"Oh Delia, I'm so glad! I was terribly worried about you."

"I wasn't really very worried," declared Delia. "I mean of course I was upset but I was quite sure Bernard was wrong. All the same it was better to get it cleared up and done with. Then I asked her about the necklace and she explained that there are two necklaces. One belonged to the old lady Bernard told us about—she died some time ago and left it to Aggie in her Will—and the other was bought in Florence for Eulalie by her husband. Of course Eulalie's necklace is much more valuable but they look much the same to anyone who doesn't know about amber. So you see that's cleared up too."

"Mrs. Winter wasn't annoyed or anything?" asked Esther in some anxiety.

"Not a bit. In fact she was pleased. She said it was friendly of me to come and tell her about it. She said she wished everyone would be open and above-board (it would save a lot of stupid misunderstandings) and she made me promise that if ever I heard anything else about her—anything horrid—I would come and tell her at once. We made a bargain that we would both do it—I mean tell each other things—so that was that."

"It was nice of her to take it like that. She sounds very sensible," said Esther thoughtfully.

"Oh, she is! She's kind, too—and clever—and very amusing. I know you think I'm silly about Eulalie but if you knew her better you would see why I like her so much."

"I'm sure I should," agreed Esther. It *did* just occur to her that, but for Delia, she might have known her new neighbour a good deal better by this time, but she was too wise—or perhaps too cowardly—to mention the fact.

This conversation with her eldest daughter comforted Esther considerably. Obviously there was no need to worry any more about Delia—that was one worry off her mind—and what was even better the conversation had been intimate and pleasant. It was a long time since she had felt so close to Delia, so much in sympathy with her.

They said good night and parted.

It was Esther's habit to read a little from her Bible every night before she went to bed. To-night she read some verses from St. Paul's Epistle to the Hebrews: "Wherefore seeing we also are compassed about with so great a cloud of witnesses, let us lay aside every weight, and the sin which doth so easily beset us, and let us run with patience the race that is set before us."

Esther knew only too well that the weight she carried was too much anxiety and her besetting sin was too little faith, so the verse was peculiarly applicable to her.

Esther was still thinking about this when she went to sleep so perhaps it was not very strange that she should dream about it. She dreamed she was running in a race. She had run races at school (indeed she had been chosen to run for her house in the school sports for she had the long slender legs of a born runner). In this dream she saw the sports-field; the green turf and the blue sky and the white ropes which marked the course, and she saw the other runners who ran beside her. There was quite a lot of people standing behind the ropes but in her dream these people were not school-friends, but the great cloud of witnesses. Esther could see them distinctly and hear them cheering her on. There was Charles of course and little Philip and her parents and her brother, who had been killed in the war, and an old aunt of whom she had been very fond, and a host of others—a cloud of witnesses!—and the knowledge that they were there, watching her and willing her to endure, lent wings to her feet.

When she awoke the dream was still vivid in her mind and it did not fade, as dreams usually do, but remained with her in all its bright colours. She had wakened before the end of the race so she never knew whether she had won, but somehow she was aware that it did not matter whether you out-ran the other competitors or came in last if you did your best and ran with courage and endurance.

CHAPTER FIFTEEN

1

THE 'fireworks' which had exploded so suddenly in the Musgrave family affected Rose least, for she had another matter to think of. She had intended to tell her mother about her meeting with Edward Steyne but there had been no opportunity and now she had changed her mind. It was so important to meet Edward (he had told her it was important) and she had a feeling that it might be difficult to convince her mother that it really was terribly important and that she must keep her appointment without fail.

There had to be some excuse for another visit to the ruins so Rose took her sketching-book and box of water-paints and set off to the rendezvous at the appointed hour. She told herself that she was not being deceitful—not really—for she intended to make some sketches of the ruins and if Edward appeared and talked to her she could not help it, could she? Edward had every right to visit the ruined Abbey. Anyone in Shepherdsford had a right to visit the place as often as they pleased. Few people did, of course. Few people felt inclined to climb the steep and stony path in the blazing hot weather . . . as a matter of fact nobody in Shepherdsford seemed so inclined. Except for Rose and Edward the ruined Abbey was deserted.

Edward was a little late in arriving at the appointed spot, but this was all to the good. By the time he arrived Rose had roughed in part of the chapel wall and a dump of willow-herb. She was so intent upon her task that she did not see Edward until he jumped down from a large block of masonry and landed on the grass at her feet.

"Oh, goodness! What a fright I got!" she exclaimed laughing.

Edward laughed too. He said, "I've been watching you for some time. You looked so sweet, sitting on that stone in your pink frock, like a rose amongst the ruins! There's a rose in the garden at Underwoods called Madame Raverie—"

"Mummie has one. She says it's an old-fashioned rose but she loves it because it has a lovely scent."

"Roses aren't proper roses without scent," declared Edward. He paused and then added, "I was dreadfully afraid you wouldn't come."

"But I promised!"

"Some people don't keep their promises."

For a moment Rose had forgotten about 'that girl'—which was horrid of her of course—but now she remembered and tried to think what to say.

"Look, Rose," Edward continued, breaking the little silence. "Look at that."

She looked and saw a small piece of silver in the palm of his hand.

"It's—it's half a sixpence!" she said in surprise. "Oh Edward, you don't mean—"

"Yes, it was a pledge. We broke it and each took half. I expect she has thrown her half away. I don't know what to do with mine."

"You ought to throw it away!"

He did so at once. It fell amongst a pile of stones and nettles making a tiny tinkling noise.

"Oh dear!" cried Rose. "I didn't mean—I mean you shouldn't have done it like that—all in a hurry—without thinking! We could never find it again—"

"I don't want to find it again."

"But perhaps you'll be sorry."

"I shan't be sorry."

The object of this meeting had been to discuss Edward's future plans but somehow there were so many other things to talk about that they did not get very far. Edward had seen a lot of the world and enjoyed telling Rose about some of his adventures. Rose had been nowhere—except St. Elizabeth's—and had seen nothing of the world so it was all very interesting. Before they knew where they were it was time for Rose to go home. "But I'll see you to-night," said Edward. "To-night?"

"Yes, I've joined the Dramatic Club. I didn't really want to but Freddie Stafford persuaded me; and when I heard you were going to be there—"

"But I don't belong to it."

"He said Miss Musgrave."

"That's Delia, my sister."

"But your sister is married—"

"Yes, but I've got two sisters," explained Rose.

"Oh goodness, if I'd known that I wouldn't have joined!" declared Edward. "I don't think I can get out of it now . . . but you'll come here to-morrow, won't you? I'll see you then."

"I don't know—" began Rose doubtfully.

"Oh, you must! We haven't settled *anything* . . . and you've got to finish your sketch."

"It doesn't matter about the sketch—"

"Doesn't it matter about me either?" asked Edward, looking at her with sad eyes. "Oh Rose, you don't know how much it means to me to talk to someone who really understands. I need a friend so badly."

Rose hesitated. "It would be all right if I could tell Mummie about it," she said doubtfully.

"But your mother knows Amie. She knows all about me," Edward pointed out. "It would be quite different if she didn't know who I was."

This was true of course.

Rose did not run home that evening. She had so much to think about that she walked home quite slowly. It had been her intention to tell her mother about Edward, but now, again, she hesitated. Would her mother understand, that was the question. How awful it would be if Mummie didn't understand and put a stop to her visits to the Abbey Woods! Poor Edward was unhappy and needed her friendship so it was right to do what she could to cheer him up . . . it couldn't be wrong. What could be wrong about meeting him and talking to him?

Besides it was so wonderful to have a friend like Edward. Some of the girls at St. Elizabeth's had talked about their 'boy-friends' and had displayed snap-shots of callow youths with untidy hair. Some of the girls had developed 'pashes' for the drawing-master or the funny little Frenchman who had come to the school three days a week to endeavour to teach them his language . . . not one of them, Rose was certain, had ever had a friend like Edward.

She wished she could write and tell Marion about her adventure in the woods and her friendship with Edward—

Marion would be thrilled to hear about it—but this was impossible of course.

2

After that Rose and Edward met at the ruined Abbey almost every afternoon. They drifted into the habit quite naturally. Rose did several sketches of the ruins, and showed them to her mother; they were not very good but Esther could not have done them to save her life so she was tremendously impressed. Esther knew that Rose had had drawing and painting lessons at school—she had paid quite a lot for them—so she was pleased that the lessons had borne fruit.

"We'll have them framed," she said.

"Oh no, they're not nearly good enough. I just do them for fun."

"I think they're wonderful," declared Esther.

Edward did not think they were wonderful; he laughed at them, but he laughed so kindly that Rose did not mind. Rose was quite ready to laugh at them herself. One day she tried to make a sketch of Edward, posed on a slab of stone, but it was a complete failure—not like him at all.

"You've given me a squint!" he exclaimed laughing heartily. "But I'll forgive you because you've given me such a beautiful crease in my trousers. Now it's my turn to have a go."

He grabbed the pencil and sketched Rose but as a matter of fact Edward was no draughtsman so his effort was not much better.

"We'll colour them," suggested Edward. "They'll look nice when they're coloured."

It was fun colouring the sketches and perhaps they *did* look a bit better, but as portraits they left much to be desired.

"Never mind," said Rose consolingly. "It's very good of my frock. You've got just the right shade of pink and all those buttons down the front and everything. It's very clever of you."

"Perhaps I could design women's dresses," said Edward looking at the sketch consideringly. "You can make a lot of money by that. I wonder if I could. I wish I could get something to do—something worth while. I'm a rolling stone, I'm afraid."

"Oh no!" Rose exclaimed.

"Yes," said Edward. "Yes, I'm a rolling stone. It isn't my fault of course. It's just because I've never been able to find a job that suited me. All I want is to find the right job and settle down and get married."

"You would have been married if that girl—"

"Yes, but she wasn't the right one. I see that now."

"You mean you're beginning to get over it?" asked Rose incredulously. "You mean you aren't feeling so miserable?"

"Not miserable at all."

Rose looked at him and discovered that he was looking at her, and there was something in his eyes which made her heart flutter.

"I must go—home," she said breathlessly.

"But it's quite early. Why must you go home so soon?"

"I must," she declared. "And—and I don't think I'll be able to—to come—any more."

Rose had got up but she could not go home because Edward was holding her hand. He said, "You must come again. Please, dear little Madame Raverie! Promise you'll come again. You're my only friend in all the world."

"Yes—well—I'll see—" said Rose incoherently.

"It all depends—"

"I shall come," he told her. "I shall be here to-morrow and if you don't come I shall be miserable."

3

There was nobody in the house when Rose got home—it was too late for tea and too early for supper—so she sat down in her mother's chair in the shade of the tree and thought about what had happened. At first she felt a little frightened and her heart still fluttered uncomfortably, but presently she began to feel better. It was silly to be frightened. There was nothing to be frightened of. Edward was lonely and needed a friend—that was all—and how lovely it was to be his friend! His only friend in all the world!

It was silly to be frightened and it would be silly not to go and meet him again—in fact it would be terribly unkind. He would be there to-morrow and if she didn't go he would be miserable. She thought of him wandering about the ruins all by himself. . . .

Rose discovered that if she shut her eyes she could see Edward. She wondered why. Perhaps it was because she had tried to draw him—if you try to draw anything you have to look at it in a very special way—but, whatever the reason, she could see Edward quite distinctly so it was strange that she had made such a botch of the sketch. Rose seized the sketch-book which was lying beside her on the ground and drew him. She did it very quickly and it really was quite good—his straight nose and his dark wavy hair—and this time she drew him in half profile so there was no danger of giving him a squint.

Yes, it was quite good, thought Rose, holding it out and looking at it with her eyes screwed up. She would show it to him to-morrow and see what he thought.

CHAPTER SIXTEEN

1

IT WAS a standing engagement for the Warrens to go to supper with the Newbiggings every Saturday evening. Sometimes they sat and talked but more often Bernard and Colonel Newbigging settled down to a game of chess. On this particular Saturday evening the two girls went out after supper and walked round the garden while the two men got down to their usual game . . . but the game did not go as usual and Bernard was mated twice within half an hour.

"What's the matter with you, Bernard?" asked the Colonel somewhat testily. "Surely you saw my Knight?"

"I'm sorry, sir," replied Bernard. "I don't seem to be able to concentrate."

"Something on your mind?"

"Yes, there is," Bernard admitted. He hesitated for a moment and then added, "I wonder—do you remember Walter Musgrave?"

"Walter Musgrave? You mean Charles's son? Yes of course I remember him. I knew him quite well. He was a good deal younger than I was but he belonged to the local cricket club—and so did I—so we saw quite a lot of each other. Walter was a very fine bowler—played for Harrow at Lords. He was all set to go up to Cambridge and then quite suddenly he disappeared and never was heard of again. You won't remember it of course—you're too young—but it caused a tremendous stir in the district."

"I don't remember it," said Bernard. "But my father-in-law told me all about it when I married Meg."

"Oh well, in that case you probably know a lot more about it than I do. There were all sorts of wild rumours at the time but nobody knew the ins and outs of the matter. Charles never spoke of it and nobody dared to ask him."

"It was a great grief to him—and to Esther too. The fact is Walter was jealous and behaved very badly. There was a frightful scene and Walter went off in the middle of the night—and vanished."

"Most extraordinary," said Colonel Newbigging.

"It must have been frightful for Charles. Everybody liked Charles."

"He was a wonderful man," Bernard agreed. "I didn't really know him until he was ill but I admired him tremendously."

They were silent for a few moments. Then Colonel Newbigging said, "Why did you ask me if I remembered Walter?"

"I wondered if you would know him if you saw him again."

"Would I know him? D'you mean he's still alive?"

Bernard nodded. "Yes, he's suddenly turned up."

"Good lord, how amazing!" exclaimed the Colonel. "It must be twenty-five years—or more! What on earth has he been doing all this time?"

"You may well ask," said Bernard smiling somewhat ruefully. "His story of what he's been doing sounds like a novel by Joseph Conrad."

"Tough, eh?"

"Tough as blazes."

"Would I know him?" said the Colonel thoughtfully. "Well that depends . . . I mean he was just a boy when I knew him, a thin gangling youth with long arms and legs, and now he must be a middle-aged man. No, I don't believe I would know him."

"Some people change and others just develop."

"What are you getting at, Bernard? D'you mean you're in doubts as to whether it really is Walter—or an impostor? Does the feller want money or something?"

"No, nothing like that," replied Bernard uncomfortably. "I'm not really in doubt, but you see I'm responsible for the family. There's nobody else and I'm Esther's trustee."

"Does Esther accept him as Walter?"

"Yes, she accepts him. She says he's quite different but she doesn't seem to have any doubts about him."

"Well, what d'you want, Bernard?"

Bernard hesitated for a moment. "I don't really know," he said slowly. "I just feel—responsible. It's worrying me a good deal. I thought I would like to tell you about it and hear your views. We don't want a lot of gossip but I know you're perfectly safe. The whole affair is so strange, so out of the ordinary, that I don't know what I ought to do."

"If you want my advice you'll have to tell me the whole thing."

"Yes. That's what I'd like. It's a long story, but if you don't mind listening—"

"Go ahead," said the Colonel. He reached for his pipe and lighted it and prepared himself to listen.

Bernard went ahead without more ado. He was glad to get the story told—and told to a man like Colonel Newbigging who had knocked about the world and knew what was what. There was nobody else with whom he could discuss the affair, except Meg of course, and Meg was too innocent and guileless to be much help. Bernard had a great respect for Colonel Newbigging; he was not exactly clever but he was full of common sense and his integrity was beyond question. So Bernard told the story' clearly and concisely from beginning to end—the mere fact of telling it helped to clear his mind—and waited for the Colonel's verdict.

"What an extraordinary tale!" exclaimed Colonel Newbigging. "Almost incredible, isn't it? But all the same I'm inclined to believe every word. If the man wanted money I should be more doubtful but you say he doesn't want money."

"Just the opposite. He's prepared to help with the repairs to Highfold Park."

"Why, I wonder."

"Well, I have a feeling he wants to clear his conscience. He knows he behaved badly and he wants to do something to make up. He didn't actually say so, but that's what I thought."

"Yes, might be that," agreed the Colonel. "Of course it doesn't make up for all the misery he caused to Charles and Esther, but at least it shows proper feeling. Are you accepting his offer?"

"Not at present—we don't need it—but we might need it later."

Colonel Newbigging was silent for a few moments and then he said, "Has Esther got any photographs of young Walter?"

"No, none. My father-in-law was so angry with Walter that he tore up all his photographs and burned them."

"Wait a minute! I believe I can help you. I've got a photograph of the Shepherdsford Cricket Eleven."

He went away and presently returned with a large photograph of eleven very serious-looking young men in long white trousers and blazers.

"There you are," he said proudly. "We were a pretty hot side—though I ses it as shouldn't—can you pick out young Walter?"

Bernard picked him out without any difficulty; he also picked out Colonel Newbigging. They looked different of course, they looked very young and defenceless—and somehow rather pathetic—but they were quite unmistakable.

"Well, there you are," said Colonel Newbigging. "Your man isn't an impostor. That's one thing settled."

"I never thought he was," declared Bernard. "But this doesn't prove his story. It's his story I want to prove."

"You can prove parts of it by writing to a firm of lawyers at the Cape. They can easily find out if Walter Musgrave is the manager of Hallsey's—which after all is the most important thing about him, isn't it?"

"Yes," agreed Bernard. "Yes, that's what I'll do." He rose and added, "Thank you very much, sir. It's a great relief to my mind—just talking about it to you. I think it's time we went home if the girls have finished their chat."

"They never finish their chat," declared Colonel Newbigging laughing. "They see each other practically every day—and what they can find to chat about beats me—but I believe they could go on chatting quite happily all night long."

2

Margaret and Sylvia had walked round the garden for a while looking at the flowers. The day had been extremely hot but it was cooler now and there was a gentle movement of air—you could hardly have called it a breeze.

"Poor flowers!" said Sylvia. "It's dreadful to see them dying for want of water. I never remember a summer like this, do you? Of course it's lovely to be able to wear thin frocks and to sit and bask in the sun—"

"If only it would rain at night," suggested Margaret. They chatted about the weather and then sat down on a wooden seat together and continued to chat.

"I wish you'd join the Dramatic Club," said Sylvia. "You like acting, don't you? Do you remember the school plays at St. Elizabeth's? I shall never forget how good you were as Portia in *The Merchant of Venice*."

"You were Nerissa—and we got the giggles in the middle of the dress rehearsal—and Miss Barton was furious with us," said Margaret giggling at the recollection of the incident.

"It was awful!" agreed Sylvia. "But we were 'all right on the night'. Listen, Meg, why don't you join the club? I wish you would. It's nonsense to say you can't leave Bernard; he could come and play chess with Daddy on club-nights."

"It isn't that, really."

"What is it then? Why won't you?"

"Because of Delia."

"Delia?"

"Yes, it isn't a sound thing to have two sisters in a small club like that—and especially two sisters who don't get on very well. There, that's the truth. Somehow I've never been able to get on very well with Delia."

"Nobody could! I mean she's terribly difficult—terribly easily offended!"

"Well, there you are!" said Margaret. "That's the reason. You see it doesn't matter so much if you aren't related to her, but when she's your sister . . ."

"But Meg—"

"And supposing—just supposing I was chosen to play some part that Delia wanted, she would be absolutely furious."

"Would it matter?"

"Yes, it would. Mummie hates rows in the family, and so do I. Besides it's Delia's Thing," continued Margaret. "It means a lot to Delia and it wouldn't mean an awful lot to me. I've got so many other things far more important. I've got Bunny and the house and lots of friends. Delia hasn't got anything. Sometimes I feel very sorry for her—it doesn't seem fair—and that helps me to bear it when she's difficult to get on with."

"Yes, I see," said Sylvia. "Yes, perhaps you're right."

"I'm glad you see," Margaret told her. "Bunny doesn't see. He doesn't understand why I put up with her 'tantrums'—as he calls them—it's the one thing Bunny and I don't agree about. He can't stand Delia at any price and won't make allowances for her. She annoys him, and then he's rude, and then—"

"Bernard rude? I can't believe it."

"You should have been at The Bridle House the other night," declared Margaret smiling somewhat ruefully. "As a matter of fact I'm glad you weren't—it was frightful. Bunny and Delia went for each other hammer and tongs and then Rose chipped in and told Delia to shut up."

"Not really!"

"Yes, really. Rose seems to have developed a mind of her own and she doesn't like it when Delia is horrid to Mummie."

"Horrid to your mother!"

"Well—yes. She is sometimes, but Mummie takes no notice. That's the best way to cope with Delia. At least I think so."

"I don't," declared Sylvia. "I think it's better to take a firm line with people like Delia—not lie down like a doormat and let them wipe their feet on you."

They were silent for a few moments and then Margaret said, "I wish to goodness somebody would marry Delia!"

"Nobody will ever marry Delia," replied Sylvia seriously. "I'm sorry to be rude about your sister but it's true. She's too—too bossy, if you know what I mean. Men don't like her. Some men are scared of her—like Mark—and other men get angry with her—like Freddie."

"Does Freddie get angry with her?"

"Yes, he's beastly to her. Honestly Meg, I don't know how she stands it—the way he speaks to her and makes fun of her before the whole club! I wouldn't stand it for a moment. I know *that*."

"Sylvia, how awful!"

"It's awful for everybody. It's so embarrassing. You don't blow what to do or where to look. I mean you don't know whether to laugh and pretend it's funny or to pretend you haven't heard. It spoils all the fun and makes a horrid sort of atmosphere."

"Poor Delia!" said Meg with a sigh.

They went on talking about Delia and about *The Mulberry Coach*. Sylvia's part in that important production was small but interesting and she had one very good scene with Giles.

"Who is Giles?" asked Margaret.

"A young man called Ernest Lake. Nobody knows him—"

"I know him!" Margaret exclaimed. "At least I've met him—a frightfully shy young man with enormous hands and feet that he doesn't know what to do with! Goodness, Sylvia, I shouldn't think he would make a very dashing villain!"

"You'd be wrong," replied Sylvia giggling. "Once Ernest gets going he's a bit too dashing. He forgets all about Ernest Lake and becomes Giles. I've still got bruises from the way he man-handled me on Wednesday night."

"Sylvia!"

"It's true—honestly. You see Giles thinks I've betrayed him—I haven't of course but that's what he thinks—so he seizes me and shakes me. We practised it several times but it wasn't very convincing. Freddie told him to put more pep into it. So then we did it again and he went for me like a gorilla and shook me until the teeth rattled in my head."

"Oh, Sylvia!"

"It's all very well to laugh," declared Sylvia. "But if he does that at an ordinary rehearsal—not even a dress rehearsal—what will he do on the night?"

They were both laughing when Colonel Newbigging and Bernard came out on to the terrace.

"What's the joke," asked the Colonel.

"Oh, you wouldn't understand," said Sylvia, wiping her eyes.

"No, you wouldn't understand," echoed Margaret.

This was slightly unfair, of course, because the Colonel would have understood perfectly—though perhaps he would not have thought it very funny.

"'Ladies Only' I suppose," said Bernard. He added, "Well, if you're finished talking we had better go home."

"Goodness, look at the time!" exclaimed Margaret glancing at her watch and rising hastily.

They all walked to the gate together.

"You'll come and see the play, won't you?" asked Sylvia. "You must all come and clap like mad." Margaret replied that wild horses wouldn't keep her away and of course Bunny would come too.

CHAPTER SEVENTEEN

1

ON THURSDAY night there was another rehearsal of *The Mulberry Coach*. It was the last which was to take place in the music room at Fairways. Next week was to be the great week for the Dramatic Club: the dress rehearsal on Wednesday and the opening night on Thursday—both in the Shepherdsford Village Hall. On Saturday the play was to be given at the Town Hall in Ernleigh. *The Mulberry*

Coach had been advertised in the local papers and already most of the reserved seats had been booked so there was no need to worry about the Club finances.

The rehearsal went off well. Even Freddie had begun to feel optimistic and doled out more encouragement than blame.

Edward Steyne had consented to 'have a go at Ralph' and Mark had surrendered the part gladly (he was now doing duty as the ancient butler and doing it well) and although Edward was not yet word-perfect he received so much help from his colleagues that his lapses were scarcely noticeable.

"I'm sorry, Freddie," said Edward when the rehearsal was over and everyone was going away. "I know I'm pretty rotten but I haven't had much time. I'll mug it up like anything before Wednesday evening—"

"You aren't rotten," declared Freddie. "You're a darn sight better than Mark, and you've galvanised Delia; she and Mark never seemed to be able lo get any life into it. I'm very grateful to you for coming to the rescue."

"I'll mug it up," repeated Edward. "It's rather fun. I'm enjoying myself. It really will be 'all right on the night', I promise you."

2

"What did you think of it?" asked Freddie when the others had left and according to custom he was helping Eulalie to set the room in order.

"It's ever so much better," she replied without hesitation. "What a difference Edward has made! It was lucky you thought of him, wasn't it? He's miles better than Mark."

"He certainly makes love to Delia much more realistically," agreed Freddie laughing. "More practised in the art—that's the reason."

"And Ernest Lake is excellent."

"Lots of pep," agreed Freddie. "You'd never think it to look at him, would you? He told me that he wants to make the stage his career. I didn't know what to say—it's a precarious sort of existence—but I believe he's got it in him and after all somebody has got to come to the top, so why not our Ernest?"

"What would his parents say?" asked Eulalie as she pushed the divan into place.

"He thinks they might agree. Apparently he has them eating out of his hand. Useful to have parents like that," added Freddie.

"Very useful. I never had any parents. I mean I can't remember them."

"Just growed—like Topsy, I suppose."

"Yes," said Eulalie, smiling inscrutably. "Just growed like Topsy."

Freddie waited but she said no more on the subject.

"Oh well," said Freddie at last. "We're all set now. I don't see what can go wrong with *The Mulberry Coach* unless somebody gets appendicitis. Shall I fetch in the tray?"

"Yes, do," said Eulalie. "It's in the usual place."

The tray was in the usual place and he carried it in as usual—and as usual they sat down together to the midnight meal; but, in spite of this, to-night seemed a little different from other nights. The conversation did not flow so spontaneously and there were several slightly uncomfortable silences.

"Look here, Eulalie," said Freddie at last. "We've had fun together, haven't we? At least it started as fun, but it isn't fun any longer."

"So we say good-bye—and no harm done."

"I didn't mean that at all. I meant it's become serious—to me."

"Serious? I don't understand."

"I think you do," he told her gravely. "You understand most things. If you want me to go on just say so."

She hesitated for a moment and then said, "Yes, you had better go on."

"Well then," said Freddie. "Well then—as I said before all this started as fun and games. We both knew the ropes, so it wasn't likely either of us would get hurt, but now it isn't fun and games any longer and I've got very badly hurt. Why don't you laugh, Eulalie?"

"It isn't funny," she said.

"Not funny?" he asked incredulously.

She shook her head. He saw with amazement that her eyes were full of tears.

"Eulalie, you really mean—"

"Yes, Freddie, I really mean it has become—serious—for me—too. Silly, isn't it?"

He had kissed her before, quite often, but this was a different kind of kiss. At last he said, "You understand, don't you? I'm in love with you—head over heels. I want to marry you. I've made love to dozens of girls and I thought I was pretty well hard-boiled, but this is a different kind of thing—altogether different—"

"Freddie, darling—yes. This is different for me too, but—"

"But what?" he asked anxiously.

"But I'll have to tell you—things."

"What sort of things? You don't mean there's any 'just cause or impediment'!" cried Freddie in alarm.

She smiled rather wanly. "I haven't got a husband in the background—if that's what you mean—but there are things you ought to know—things about me. I don't want to tell you—"

"Then don't tell me!"

"I think I must."

"But, my dearest girl, why should you? I've knocked about a bit myself and done things I don't like to think of. I should hate to tell you a detailed story of my life."

"I should hate to hear it."

"Well then, let bygones be bygones."

For a few moments she hesitated and then she said, "No, I couldn't do that. I couldn't marry you without telling you. Supposing you heard things about me from someone else!"

"I don't care what you've done!" exclaimed Freddie ardently.

"Not now, perhaps—"

"Not ever!"

"I can't risk it," she declared. "I might have risked it, but I happen to know there's someone here in Shepherdsford who is a little too interested in my history."

"Eulalie, what on earth do you mean?"

"You'll see," she told him. "I shall have to start at the beginning. It's a long story and it may bore you frightfully but I can't help that."

"Bore me?"

"Well, no," she admitted. "I said that without thinking. You won't be bored."

"You're frightening me horribly," said Freddie gravely.

"I'm frightening myself," she replied. "Perhaps when you've heard it you'll never want to speak to me again."

3

There was a short silence and then Eulalie said, "I wonder if you remember telling me I was 'a born actress'. It's true,

Freddie. I've been acting all my life—not acting on the stage, but acting in real life—pretending to be different from what I really am."

"We all do that!"

"Most of us, I suppose, but I've done it to such an extent that I don't know where to find the real me."

"You're Eulalie. That's all that matters."

"I'm not," she said seriously. "My name isn't Eulalie. I very nearly told you the first time we met—that first evening. I had a sudden crazy impulse to tell you—just to see what you would say. I began life as Agatha."

"It's quite a good name!"

"Yes, but I was Aggie, you see. Not quite so good, is it?"

"Well, perhaps—"

"Aggie was a poor miserable creature with carroty hair and ugly sticking-out teeth—"

"Eulalie!" exclaimed Freddie looking at her in bewilderment. "What's all this nonsense? I don't understand."

"I'm trying to tell you, but it isn't easy, and you're making it much more difficult. You must sit back and listen or I shan't be able to go on. Listen, Freddie: Aggie was plain. Her best friend couldn't have described her otherwise. Her only asset was a good figure and that wasn't much use without good clothes to show it off."

"I don't know what you're talking about!"

"I'm talking about Aggie. She was a typist to begin with but she was such a bad typist that she kept on getting the sack and at last the woman in the agency got sick of finding jobs for her and suggested she should take a post as companion to an elderly lady who lived in Chester. I discovered afterwards that Mrs. Frome had worn out five companions in a year. If I had known this at the time I wouldn't have taken the job . . . or perhaps I would. I hadn't much choice, really.

"I was told that there was a cook-housekeeper—and so there was—but she left the day after I arrived, and when Mrs. Frome found I could cook she didn't bother to look for another. There was a good deal to do; Mrs. Frome was lame and needed quite a lot of attention; she liked to be read to—I used to read old-fashioned romances for hours on end. She was a 'difficult' old lady, crotchety and rather mean. She paid me two pounds a week for my services!"

"Why on earth did you stay?" cried Freddie. "Surely you could have got something else!"

"It was—safe," said Eulalie slowly. "I think that was the reason I stuck it. The house was warm and I had plenty of food; that was enough—to begin with. But you mustn't keep on interrupting, Freddie."

"All right, go on—if you must."

"Mrs. Frome had a son," continued Eulalie. "He was married and had some sort of business in Liverpool. They came and saw Mrs. Frome from time to time. Sometimes they took us both out in their car for a drive. He had one of those big American cars and liked to drive fast. He did it to show off. I didn't like it much, neither did Mrs. Frome—but when he saw we were scared he drove faster. That was the sort of man he was."

"Not a very pleasant sort of chap!"

Eulalie took no notice of the interruption. "The Peter Fromes came to tea occasionally but he and his mother got on very badly and every time they came there was a quarrel. Usually I was sent out of the room so that they could quarrel more comfortably, but quite often they forgot that I was there. You see Aggie was a self-effacing creature—she was plain and dowdy—she wasn't the sort of woman you would look at twice."

Eulalie said this with a bitter emphasis which was very distressing to Freddie.

"Oh, Eulalie, you're upsetting yourself—and me too! Is it necessary?"

"Yes, I'm afraid so. The story gets more interesting later on. I'm just setting the scene. You've got to realise what it was like living in that dull little house with that crotchety old lady before you can understand. After a bit I felt I couldn't bear it any longer; I felt as if I were in prison. The only time I got out was to do the shopping and to exercise the dog . . . so I told Mrs. Frome I must go. I didn't think she would mind a bit, but she was quite upset. She had got used to me; she was quite fond of me in her own queer way."

Eulalie hesitated for a few moments and then continued. "She was lonely. It was her own fault of course. If she had been pleasant and agreeable she could have had lots of friends but she wasn't pleasant and agreeable. The only creature that loved her was the dog. He was a Scotch terrier, old and fat and snappy. They were both old and fat and snappy—but they loved each other. When Scottie died Mrs. Frome was broken-hearted. Soon after that her son came to see her, but instead of being sympathetic about Scottie he tried to persuade her that it was all for the best. He said he would buy her another dog. This was quite the wrong thing to say—"

"Why are you telling me all this?" asked Freddie. "What has it got to do with us?"

"Quite a lot," replied Eulalie. "It was after Scottie died that I had my big idea. I had always wanted to travel and see the world. I read every travel book I could get hold of and I used to dream of all the places I wanted to see. I wish I could make you understand what I felt about travelling. It was a passion—a sort of mania. The years were passing and

I hadn't seen anything. I was stuck in that dull little house with no hope of escape. Then suddenly when Scottie died I saw my chance so I began to work on Mrs. Frome. It was a long dreary winter and she had a touch of bronchitis—that helped a lot. I began to drop hints about sunshine and blue skies in the South of France. You see I knew her pretty well by this time so I knew how to go about it, I knew exactly what to say. Quite soon she began to think it was her own idea to go abroad. Of course Peter Frome and his wife were horrified when they heard about the plan. They came to see her and I was sent out of the room—"

"I suppose they persuaded her not to go?"

"They tried to, of course, but the more they went on about it the more determined she became. They didn't understand her at all. It was no good trying to persuade Mrs. Frome to do anything; she had to be managed very carefully indeed. There was a frightful row that afternoon—the worst ever. I heard all about it after they had gone: what Peter had said and what Ethel had said and what Mrs. Frome had replied. 'They don't want me to spend the money,' she declared. 'I'll spend my money how I please—and they needn't think they'll get a penny when I die. I shall leave it to a dogs' home.' I pretended to be doubtful about it and advised her to change her mind—that clinched the matter. I knew it would.

"I expect you think it was horrible of me—perhaps it was—but Peter Frome had always treated me like dirt and he wasn't very kind to his mother either. He could have done a lot more for the old lady (he could have taken a little trouble and sent her a present occasionally; she would have appreciated a little attention) so it was really his own fault. At least that was what I felt about it."

"It seems to me they were all exceedingly nasty," declared Freddie. "There wasn't much to choose between them. Did you take the old woman to the South of France?"

Eulalie laughed. "We spread our wings much wider than that. We decided to go to America and then on through the Panama Canal to the Pacific but when we consulted a Travel Agency Mrs. Frome was so horrified at the price of the tickets that she began to waver. I suggested she should go without me but of course she couldn't have gone alone. We talked about it constantly and at last I said I would go with her 'as a friend'. She would have to pay my fare, I couldn't manage that, but she needn't pay me my salary. It was a silly idea, really, because my wretched two pounds a week wouldn't have made the slightest difference to her but my offer turned the scale. 'Can you afford it?' she asked in surprise.

I told her the truth. I said I had nearly two hundred pounds in the bank but not another penny to my name. 'In that case you can't afford it!' she exclaimed. I told her that I didn't care. I wanted to go with her and look after her. We shillied and shallied for days but by this time she was so keen to go 'just to show Peter' that we came to an agreement. I would go with her and use my own money for necessary expenses over and above my fare and she would leave me some money in her Will to make up.

"We made a joke of it—or at least she made a joke of it—she had a grim sense of humour. 'I'm a good life,' she said. 'D'you know what that means, Aggie? It means I may outlive you unless you put poison in my coffee.'"

Freddie had got up and was prowling up and down like a restless tiger. "I wouldn't have blamed you," he said.

"Well, I didn't, anyhow," declared Eulalie with a mirthless laugh. "If that's what's worrying you. Come and sit down, Freddie, you're making me jittery."

Freddie came and sat down. "So you set off on your travels?"

Eulalie nodded. "Yes, but before we started she went to her lawyer and altered her Will. 'You won't lose by it, Aggie,' she said when she came home. 'You'll get your money back and perhaps a little bit extra.' That was all I wanted, so off we went.

"I told you she wasn't easy to get on with but I was used to fetching things for her and being ordered about and snapped at so I didn't mind. I would have put up with a lot more if it had been necessary. I was 'seeing the world' at last, so I didn't care how much I had to put up with. Mrs. Frome enjoyed it almost as much as I did, not for the sake of seeing the world—she didn't care a button about all the wonderful things we saw—but she liked the warmth and the comfort and she liked chatting to the other passengers. We had a marvellous trip. We did all we had planned—and more. We were away for nearly six months.

"Then we went back to Chester. When we got home Peter and his wife came and saw her; the quarrel was made up and they stayed and had tea. This time I wasn't banished from the room. Mrs. Frome was more dependent on me than before, she had begun to lose her memory and she liked me to be there to help her out. She started to tell the Peter Fromes some of our experiences and forgot what she wanted to say. 'Tell them, Aggie,' she said. 'I can't remember that woman's name—the woman with the red hair that we met in Honolulu.' Later she said, 'We had a good time, didn't we Aggie?' She kept on drawing me into the conversation. I was sent to fetch the picture-postcards and to find her spectacles, I was asked to pour out tea. It was then that they saw the red light."

4

Freddie had been getting a trifle bored with the story (there seemed to be no point in it) but now he sat up and showed more interest.

"Was she doing it on purpose?" he asked. "Did she mean to frighten them?"

"Oh yes," said Eulalie, nodding. "She was like that, you see. She enjoyed making mischief; it amused her to give people a little prick and watch them squirm. She had that queer streak in her."

"What an absolute gorgon!"

"No, not really," said Eulalie thoughtfully. "Lots of people have that queer streak in their natures. It's their way of 'getting their own back'."

"Dangerous," commented Freddie.

"Yes, mischief making is always dangerous—more or less. It's playing about with gunpowder."

"Was there an explosion?"

"Not in the way you mean. After that day the Peter Fromes behaved quite differently. They came to see Mrs. Frome more often and brought her flowers and there were no more rows. She saw through it, of course. She laughed when she saw the flowers and said Peter was 'sucking up'. Then they asked her to go and stay with them for Christmas. 'Not without Aggie', she said. As a matter of fact she couldn't have gone without me; she was becoming more and more helpless; but the Peter Fromes didn't know this so they tried to persuade her to come alone—but they had to have Aggie."

Eulalie paused. She was silent for so long that Freddie could not bear it. "What happened at the Christmas Party?" he asked at last. "There couldn't have been much festivity about it."

"There wasn't a Christmas Party. There was an accident."

"An accident?"

"Yes. Peter Frome came to fetch us in his car. There had been frost in the night and the road was slippery—I told you he drove fast. He was overtaking a brewer's dray when it happened."

"What happened?"

"I don't know, really. I can't tell you much about it except that the car skidded across the road and overturned. These things happen every day of course, but somehow you never think about them happening to *you*. We were all injured. Mrs. Frome had a fractured femur; Peter had several broken ribs; I was knocked out completely. I came to in hospital, bruised and cut and my teeth knocked to pieces—you never saw such a mess! At first I was too ill to know or care what had happened to the others.

"Peter got off lightly. His ribs were strapped up and he was sent home, but Mrs. Frome developed pneumonia. After a few days they came and hauled me out of bed and took me in to see her—she had been asking for me constantly—but by that time it was too late; she didn't even know me. They told me to speak to her but it was no use."

"She died?"

Eulalie nodded. "She died that night . . . and she left her money to Aggie."

"All of it?"

"Yes, every penny. Everything she possessed."

"Great Scott!" exclaimed Freddie.

For a few moments there was silence.

"Great Scott!" repeated Freddie. "The Peter Fromes must have been mad with rage."

"Yes, they were furious. At first they tried to frighten me and make me 'go shares', but I wouldn't. Why should I? The old lady had left it to me, so obviously she wanted me to have it. Then they said she was in her dotage and I had 'used undue influence' and made her change her Will in my favour. In a way it was true of course. I had toiled and moiled for her, night and day . . . and she certainly wouldn't have gone abroad if I hadn't 'influenced' her."

"She enjoyed it—"

"Oh yes, but that wasn't the reason I made her go. You see, Freddie," said Eulalie thoughtfully. "You see, when a thing like that happens it's very difficult to judge one's own motives. To be quite honest I wouldn't have stood her bad temper if I hadn't hoped she would leave me something when she died. I never thought for a moment she would leave me all she possessed!"

"You thought Peter would get it?"

"No, I knew he wouldn't. I thought it would go to a dogs' home; that's what she always said. When she was annoyed with me she used to say, 'You needn't think you'll get a fortune when I die. You'll get what I promised—and no more. Peter won't get it either. I've left it to a dogs' home because of Scottie. Scottie was the only creature that ever loved me . . .' Sometimes when she was in one of her moods she went on like that for hours."

"I don't know how you bore it!"

Eulalie did not answer that. She hurried on with her story. "They took the case to court. Oh Freddie, it was an absolute nightmare! I can scarcely bear to think of it even now. I was besieged by reporters wanting interviews, wanting to take photographs of me, there were headlines in the papers—perhaps you remember the case?"

He shook his head.

"Lots of people did—some people still remember it," declared Eulalie somewhat incoherently. "It made such a stir at the time. It was all so horrible. They produced witnesses—people that I scarcely knew—who stood up and said I had wormed my way into her affections. Some of the things they said were absolute lies, some were partly true and difficult to deny. It's far more difficult to deny a thing if it's partly true—or just twisted. Fortunately I had briefed a good lawyer, he was young but extremely clever and he was mad keen to win the case—but it was touch and go. Half-way through I thought it was hopeless, all the evidence seemed against me. I wondered what I was going to do if I lost the case.

I hadn't a single farthing; I was in debt to the tune of over a hundred pounds. I was desperate. Then, when I went into the witness box, the whole atmosphere changed—I could feel it change. Mr. Cunliffe had told me what to say but it wasn't so much what I said, it was what I looked like, dejected and dowdy with a scarred face and broken teeth! Mr. Cunliffe played up the accident for all he was worth (it had been proved already that Peter Frome had been driving recklessly). As a matter of fact the accident had nothing to do with the point at issue—even I could see that—but all the same it turned the scale.

"When the case was decided in my favour I was so exhausted, so down and out, that I scarcely cared. The Cunliffes were very kind to me, they had me to stay with them and looked after me. Mrs. Cunliffe was an American, very young and attractive, with that well-groomed appearance that the best American women have. When I had recovered a little she made me go straight off to America and gave me an introduction to a cousin in Chicago who ran a clinic—it was a sort of super nursing-home. They put me to bed and got to work on me: there was a plastic surgeon and a dermatologist and a dentist and several other specialists of different sorts and kinds. There was a great deal to be done. The scars on my face hadn't healed properly and my teeth were in a terrible condition. I had several operations and a long course of treatment, it was all very unpleasant. It cost the earth, but fortunately that didn't matter . . . and it was worth every penny. When I came out of that place I was an entirely different creature. Aggie had vanished for ever."

Thinking back, Eulalie remembered how extraordinary it had been to feel and look an entirely different creature; to see people turning their heads to look at her, not in pity but in admiration; to have as much money as she needed, and to wear pretty clothes. At first she felt shy about her changed appearance but soon she was able to face the world with assurance, and learned to walk into a crowded restaurant as if it belonged to her.

"You were Eulalie," said Freddie, who had been watching her face.

"Yes."

"Where did you meet George Winter?"

"Goodness, Freddie, haven't you had enough? I met George in Santa Barbara. I had gone there after I left the clinic to complete my cure. George was much older than I was, and terribly delicate, but we soon became friends and went about together a good deal. I told him some of my history, but not all by any means. Then one day he asked me to marry him. We weren't madly in love but we had both been through a bad time. We understood each other perfectly, George and I. He knew I wanted to change my name and cast off my old life completely and I knew he wanted companionship and care. It sounds a cold-blooded sort of bargain, but it wasn't really; we both got exactly what we wanted—at any rate I'm not ashamed of it. Of course we shouldn't have come home. George wasn't fit to stand the climate, he might have lived some years longer if we had stayed in Santa Barbara, but he wanted to come home more than anything; he could talk of nothing else. So we waited until the Spring and then came home. We stayed at a hotel in Torquay. For a time George's health improved and we were able to go about and enjoy ourselves. He helped me to choose new clothes—the sort of clothes that suited me. I told you he had good taste in clothes."

"And that amber necklace," Freddie reminded her.

"No, not really. It belonged to Mrs. Frome. I'm afraid I tell lies quite often," said Eulalie frankly.

"So do I," admitted Freddie. "It would be ghastly to be married to a woman who couldn't tell a lie."

She looked at him in amazement. "Freddie, does that mean—does it mean you don't mind—about Aggie?"

"Why should I mind?"

"I thought Aggie might—might put you off."

He hesitated for a moment and then said, "I'm sorry for Aggie. She had a raw deal hadn't she? I wouldn't have blamed Aggie if she had poisoned that old woman. That ghastly old woman was simply asking to be poisoned."

"You're talking nonsense, Freddie."

"Well, perhaps," admitted Freddie. "Poisoning *is* rather beastly—but we're getting side-tracked, aren't we? The point is I never knew Aggie. You seem to have been telling me the history of a totally unknown woman."

"You mean it doesn't put you off—knowing about Aggie?" asked Eulalie incredulously.

"Why should it put me off? Aggie has nothing whatever to do with you and me."

"Oh, Freddie! Is that—really—how you feel? It hasn't made any—difference?"

"Any difference? Why should it? I still love you—if that's what you mean—I still want to marry you. Darling, it's you I love. It's Eulalie. Here, I say! What on earth are you crying about?"

"I don't know," she declared hysterically. "I don't know what I'm—crying about. It seems too good to be true."

5

It was late when at last Freddie went home. They had talked for hours but there was still so much to say that they lingered on the doorstep. It was broad daylight and the birds were singing but there was nobody about. Everybody in Shepherdsford, except themselves, was asleep.

Their plans were made. Neither of them wanted a fuss; they would 'creep away furtively, hand-in-hand,' and be married in London. Freddie was due a holiday, so they could go abroad for a month by which time the surprise and excitement of Shepherdsford would have died down a little. Meantime there was the play—next week—they were both looking forward to the play.

"It will be fun," said Freddie.

"But we must be careful," Eulalie reminded him, putting a finger to her lips with an exaggerated gesture of secrecy.

"Yes, we must be *very* careful," agreed Freddie smiling. He took the finger and kissed it fondly.

When Freddie had gone Eulalie locked up the house and went to bed. She was very tired, for she had gone through an emotional upheaval, but she was happier than she had ever been in all her life.

Chapter Eighteen

1

WALTER Musgrave had written to announce his arrival in Shepherdsford on Saturday and to confirm his invitation to all the members of the Musgrave family to luncheon on Sunday at The Owl. Esther had received a letter from him—so had Delia and Margaret and Rose—Walter was anxious to do things correctly. Esther's letter explained that Walter had been delayed so he would be spending only two nights at The Owl; he would have to go back to London on Monday to finish up his business affairs before flying home. He would like to drop in at The Bridle House on Saturday night after supper to discuss a matter of family business.

Naturally Esther wondered what he wanted to discuss. She asked Bernard, but Bernard did not know. However Bernard told her that he had made inquiries about Walter through a firm of lawyers at the Cape and they had reported that Walter Musgrave was sound. He had a very good position in Hallsey's and in fact was all and more than he had claimed to be.

Esther had never thought of doubting Walter's word, but she realised that Bernard had been wise to make inquiries.

When Walter called the girls were out—they had gone off together to play tennis—so Esther was alone. She had not told them he was coming for Walter had made it clear that the matter he wanted to discuss was private.

The evening was warm so they sat in the garden and after a few opening remarks Walter came straight to the point.

"Do you think Delia would like to come out with me to the Cape?" he asked.

"What!" exclaimed Esther in blank amazement.

"I thought you might be surprised," said Walter smiling. "I haven't mentioned it to Delia, and of course if you don't like the idea we'll say no more about it."

"You want to take Delia with you—to the Cape!"

"That's the idea."

"But—but why?"

Walter laughed. "That's easily answered. I need a housekeeper and Delia would be all the better for a job."

"Oh!" said Esther doubtfully. "Oh Walter—I don't know. It isn't a thing to decide all in a hurry—"

"I'm afraid it is," he replied. "I'm afraid it must be decided in a hurry. It would be much better for Delia to come home with me so that I can look after her on the journey—much better than coming out later alone."

"But we can't decide until we've thought it over."

"Look, Esther," he said. "I know this seems a bit sudden but honestly it's a sensible plan. Delia is twenty-six, she's wasting her time in Shepherdsford—just playing about and doing nothing useful. What Delia needs is a woman-size job of work. It would do her good to see a bit of the world. I'll take care of her I promise you. I think we'd get on all right but if she doesn't like it she can come home to you in six months." He hesitated and then added, "I'll pay for everything of course. She'll have to get clothes—you could have a few days together in London—and I'll give her an allowance. In return she'll run the bungalow for me and manage the indoor staff."

"But—but—"

"But me no buts!" exclaimed Walter laughing. "Of course Delia may not want to come. I just want your permission to ask her, that's all."

"I can't decide now," declared Esther. "You must wait until to-morrow. That will do, won't it?"

Walter said it would.

This was no new idea of Walter's—no sudden whim. He had been thinking about it off and on ever since his last visit to Shepherdsford. He had been thinking about this half-sister who carried a chip on her shoulder and he had come to the conclusion that she was very like himself. Perhaps they had both inherited the propensity for chip-carrying from some unknown Musgrave forebear.

Walter had some knowledge of psychology and, being interested, he had observed the family carefully and come to certain conclusions—the photograph album had helped considerably. Delia was the eldest. She had been petted and perhaps a little spoiled until Margaret had arrived—and then Philip. After that, as was only natural, the other children had shared the love and attention which had been lavished upon Delia alone. All this could be seen from the little pictures in the photograph album. Already, at five years old, you could see the droop of resentment at the corners of Delia's pretty little mouth. From then on Delia had been 'difficult'.

Margaret had always been 'easy'. Margaret had charm—that elusive quality so difficult to define but immediately recognisable—she had a sweet sunny nature, 'everyone liked Meg,' Margaret had made 'lots of friends at school'—so Walter had been told. Nothing had been said of Delia's friends so presumably she had few. People who went about the world with chips on their shoulders were usually friendless—as Walter was aware.

Delia had seen her younger sister loved and admired, she had watched her being married (pretty clothes, thought Walter, and then the wedding, everyone clustering round the bride). Last, but not least, *there* was Margaret in a new house, built for her by an adoring husband, possessing everything that the heart of woman could desire.

It might be said that Delia ought to have been able to rise above her feelings and take all this in her stride but Walter knew from bitter experience that if you happen to be 'made that way' it is not easy to rise above your feelings.

He had explained his reasons for his invitation quite frankly. He had told Esther that he wanted a house-keeper and Delia would be all the better for a woman-size job, but there was another reason for the invitation which he had not revealed—nor did he intend to reveal it. Walter felt that if he could be helpful to Delia, who was his father's daughter, he would be making amends, to some extent at least, for the way he had behaved and the suffering he had caused all those years ago.

2

Walter's luncheon party took place on the following day. He had been doubtful about having it on a Sunday, and giving the proprietors of The Owl so much extra work, but Mrs. Palmer had replied that Sunday was the only day she could undertake it. She would have to get girls from the village to help her and they were all fully employed during the week. Mrs. Palmer had cast her eye round the various girls she knew and had decided upon Daphne and Flo Bloggs and Violet Danks. With these three staunch supporters Mrs. Palmer felt she could face the luncheon-party with equanimity. She had no doubt that the girls would accept the assignment, and of course she was right. Anything 'different' or 'out of the usual' was fun . . . "and the extra money'll come in useful," said Violet gleefully.

The three staunch supporters arrived at The Owl shortly after eleven and were put to work immediately on various preparations. Mrs. Palmer chose Daphne to help her in the kitchen, the other two would serve the meal . . . not in the dining-room but in a large room on the first floor. Long ago, when The Owl was a coaching inn, this room had been used as a coffee-room for the stage-coach passengers, it was never used now. It had a vast fireplace and a floor which sloped down to one corner and huge beams across the ceiling. It was a grim sort of room with a musty smell, but when the windows had been opened and the furniture polished and vases of flowers had been placed in position it cheered up wonderfully.

"It don't look so bad," suggested Flo.

"Looks quite pretty," agreed Violet.

3

Walter was ready for his guests in good time. He surveyed all the preparations and approved of them. He was determined that his party should be a success. Walter was putting the last little touches to the table when Esther arrived; she was the first.

"Walter," she said in a low voice. "I've been thinking about your plan. I've 'slept on it'—or rather I've lain awake on it—and I've made up my mind that we ought to accept your offer."

"I'm glad!" exclaimed Walter. "I'm sure it's the right thing—and you mustn't worry, Esther. You won't worry will you?"

"No, I won't," she replied. "I worry too much about things, but I made up my mind that it doesn't do any good. You've just got to do the best you can and 'run the race with patience'."

Walter looked somewhat bewildered.

"It was just a dream I had," explained Esther smiling a little. "It was a very vivid dream, but I'm not going to tell you about it. There's nothing so boring as other people's dreams. Besides we've got to discuss your plan for Delia. I haven't said anything about it to anyone, because you told me not to . . . and of course Delia must decide herself whether she wants to go with you or not. I just wanted to tell you that I think it's a good plan and I shan't put any difficulties in the way if Delia wants to go. You'll ask her yourself, I suppose."

"Yes, I'll ask her after lunch. There's no time to waste. You realise that I'm flying home on Thursday."

"Thursday! Do you mean you want Delia to go with you on Thursday?" exclaimed Esther in amazement.

"Yes, I've got a seat in the plane for her. I booked it just in case—"

"Thursday is impossible!" cried Esther.

"Nothing is impossible," declared Walter laughing.

No more could be said about the matter, for the two girls—Vi and Flo—were coming in and out of the room all the time, and a few moments later the other members of the party arrived.

It was an excellent lunch. There was nothing elaborate about it but everything was well cooked, everything tasted delicious. They started with consommé julienne, slightly chilled, and went on to roast lamb with green peas and mint jelly. For a sweet course there was gooseberry pie and slabs of home-made ice-cream.

The conversation was cheerful and friendly, Walter kept the ball rolling with tact and diplomacy.

Esther did not say much, for in spite of her determination not to worry she could not help being somewhat apprehensive. It was one thing to give permission for Delia to go to South Africa at some future date but quite another to discover that a seat had been booked on a plane in three days' time . . . three weeks would scarcely be enough to get used to the idea and to make all the necessary preparations! Esther had said it was impossible—and of course it was—but all the same she had a feeling that Walter was the sort of person who usually got his own way about things; he was used to making instant decisions and rushing about the world here there and everywhere. Walter was the sort of person who would pack a suitcase and start off to Canada or Timbuktu or New Zealand without turning a hair . . . and this being so, was he the sort of person who could be trusted to take proper care of Delia?

Coming back from these uncomfortable reflections Esther discovered that the conversation was still running smoothly. Managing the conversation was usually her job when she had all her family seated round the same table—but it was not her job to-day. Walter was the host, and Walter was managing her difficult family with the greatest of ease. Without saying very much himself he was making them all talk, nobody was left to sit in silence. Esther, who was somewhat addicted to cliches, thought of 'an iron hand within a velvet glove' and wondered how he and Delia would get on—if Delia decided to go.

(Oh dear, thought Esther, here I am worrying again, after making up my mind not to worry . . . and anyhow, what could I have done except give him my permission to ask Delia?)

When they had finished lunch they sat at the table and chatted. There were walnuts, but The Owl Inn was unable to produce nut-crackers, so Walter gave a further exhibition of 'the iron hand' by cracking them quite easily in his fingers and distributing them to his guests—a feat which impressed his guests considerably.

"Goodness, Walter, how strong you are!" exclaimed Rose in admiring tones.

"Bunny can do it, too," said Margaret quickly.

"But not like that," declared Bernard. "I can crack two together but not one alone. How on earth do you do it?"

"Oh, it's just a knack," replied Walter smiling. "Look, you hold it like this and give it a sudden squeeze—and there you are."

Soon they were all laughing and trying to crack the walnuts, but in spite of being shown 'the knack' nobody could accomplish the feat—not even Bernard.

4

Walter had said he would ask Delia after lunch, so presently he rose and said, "Come on, Delia. Let's walk down to the river together. I want to talk to you."

"To me?" asked Delia in surprise.

"Yes, to you. The others will excuse us, I hope."

"Yes, of course," said Esther nodding. "We'll wait for you. There's no hurry for us to go home."

The garden behind the Inn stretched down to the river and to the ford which had given Shephersford its name. The river was very low after the dry weather, it was scarcely more than a trickle wending its way between stones and boulders, and the ford was a bed of gravel. Walter had been sufficiently interested in the history of the ford to ask the Palmers about it and had got a good deal of information from them. At any other time he would have told Delia about the shepherds who had used it long ago, bringing their packs of wool from the hills and crossing the river on their way to the market. Today, however, there were other things to talk about and Waller came straight to the point and put his proposition into words.

"Come with you to South Africa!" exclaimed Delia incredulously. "What an extraordinary idea!"

"I see nothing extraordinary about it," Walter replied calmly. "It seems a very sensible idea to me."

"Walter, you don't really mean it!"

"Of course I mean it. Do you think I would say it if I didn't mean it? That would be a stupid thing to do."

She gazed at him, wide-eyed.

"Listen, Delia. It's a sensible plan. I want a house-keeper and you want a job. It's a simple as that."

It did not sound very simple to Delia. She said doubtfully, "But—but I don't want a job. At least—"

"Of course you want a job. There's nothing for you to do in Shepherdsford. You're just wasting your time here, aren't you? I've heard you say Shepherdsford was dull—"

"It's as dull as ditchwater!"

"Well then, here's your chance to get out of it."

By this time they had found a dilapidated seat in the neglected garden, so they sat down together and Walter began to explain the matter fully. He told her what sort of life she might expect if she decided to accept his invitation; he reminded her of the little slides he had shown her—the pictures of his bungalow on the Hallsey estate. "It's a good life out there," he told her. "I've got a lot of friends—the Hallseys are delightful people—hut don't imagine it would be a sinecure, Delia. You'd have to pull your weight. I want a housekeeper; I want someone to make things run smoothly."

"I don't know much about housekeeping."

"You could learn, couldn't you? It wouldn't take you long to learn the ropes. I've got quite a good staff but the 'boys' are apt to take liberties with a bachelor. You would have to manage them and keep them in order."

"I don't know if I could."

"Of course you could. You're no fool. If other people can do it so can you."

She was silent.

"What's your alternative?" he asked impatiently. "Are you content to remain here for the rest of your life—doing nothing? It seems a pretty grim prospect to me."

"Oh Walter!"

"Well, there you are. That's your choice, Delia. I asked your mother and she said you must make your own decision—"

"Oh, of course Mummie would be only too glad to get rid of me!"

"Is that fair?"

"Fair?" echoed Delia in surprise.

"Do you think she ought to have turned down my offer without consulting you?"

"No, of course not!"

Walter smiled. "Well then, you're being unjust to her, aren't you? You're being unreasonable."

"I suppose I am," muttered Delia, looking somewhat ashamed.

"If you don't want to come say so."

"Of course I want to come! I've always wanted to travel. I've always wanted to get away from this mouldy little place and see the world . . . if only it hadn't been such a rush."

"It is a bit of a rush," admitted Walter. "I'm sorry about that but I couldn't help it. I tried to get a seat for you in the plane but there wasn't one to be had. They only let me know on Friday that there had been a cancellation. That's the reason I said nothing about it before."

"But Walter, I shall have to get clothes, and I don't see how—"

"Yes, you must get clothes," he agreed. "You'll wants lots of pretty dresses. You had better come up to town with your mother and get all you need. I shall pay for them of course. A couple of hundred ought to be enough."

"A couple of hundred pounds!" asked Delia, unable to believe her ears.

"I want you to do me credit. I shall want you to receive my friends and come to parties with me. The social side of my job is rather important and a pretty sister with pretty dresses will be a great asset—see?"

She turned her head and smiled at him. "Oh Walter!"

"Come on, be a sport, Delia! It's now or never. Which is it to be?"

She took a deep breath and said, "It's now."

Walter nodded, "That's right. I'm sure you won't regret it; not if I can help it, anyhow."

"We had better go and tell the others," cried Delia, leaping from the seat and running up the path to the inn.

Walter followed more slowly and found her surrounded by her family—they were all talking at once—but although they were all excited Walter noticed that they were not surprised and he realised that Esther must have told them why he had wanted to speak to Delia alone.

"You've decided to go," Margaret was saying. "I'm sure you're right."

"It seems an excellent plan," declared Bernard.

"It would be silly to miss such a chance!" cried Rose.

"If you don't like it you can come home," said Esther who was still somewhat doubtful. "Of course you can't go on Thursday, there isn't time, but perhaps—"

"I must be ready by Thursday. Walter has booked my seat on the plane."

"It will be a rush," said Bernard. "But I don't see why you couldn't manage it."

"We'll manage it somehow," said Margaret. "We can all help, can't we?"

"Thursday!" cried Esther. "It's only three days!"

"You'll have to go up to town to-morrow," Margaret told her.

"To-morrow! We can't possibly—"

"You must, Mummie. Delia will have to get clothes."

"Lots of clothes!" cried Delia. "Walter says so."

"Why can't you go up to town to-morrow, Esther?" asked Bernard in calm reasonable tones. "We can shut up the house for you and make all the necessary arrangements and Rose can come and stay with us while you're away."

"Yes, that's the best plan," Margaret agreed.

"The milk—" began Esther feebly. "The milk will have to be cancelled—and the bread—and the papers—"

"Milk and bread and papers!" exclaimed Delia scornfully. "How silly you are! Don't you realise that this is the chance of a lifetime? What does it matter about milk and bread and papers?"

"It will be all right," said Margaret tactfully. "I'll see to everything. All you have to do is to pack what you need for three days in town. You can do that, can't you, Mummie?"

"I'll help you to pack," said Rose.

Walter stood and listened. They were all being very kind and helpful, but he could not help feeling sorry for Delia. Did she realise that her family was rather too pleased at the prospect of her departure? Perhaps not . . . perhaps her family did not realise this either . . . perhaps it was merely a subconscious reaction to the sudden plan.

"You can do that, can't you, Mummie?" repeated Margaret. "You can be ready to go to town to-morrow by the afternoon train?"

"I suppose so," said Esther with a sigh. All at once she felt old and silly. She was a back number, unfit for the Modern World. This was not the way things had been done when she was young. In those days—which seemed far off to Esther—people had laid their plans at leisure and made careful preparations. Nobody would have thought of dashing off to the ends of the earth at a moment's notice.

As they went down the steps to the cars, which were standing in the court-yard of the inn, Bernard took her arm and said in a low voice, "Don't worry, Esther. It's the best thing for Delia. There's no future for her here in Shepherdsford. You know that, don't you? And if she's going it's better for her to go in a hurry like this without thinking about it too much."

"You are a comfort to me, Bernard," said Esther rather shakily.

5

Esther and Delia went off together to London in a whirl of confusion and it was not until they were actually seated in the train that Esther remembered the play.

"I thought the play was this week," she said. "I suppose you remembered to tell Freddie Stafford you won't be there."

"Oh, they'll get someone else to play Angela," replied Delia casually. "It's a pity after learning the part but it couldn't be helped."

Delia had not answered her mother's question. She had not told Freddie. She had thought of ringing him up and then had decided to write to him from London instead.

Freddie would be angry so it would be much easier to write from London.

Delia had abandoned *The Mulberry Coach*. She did not care what happened to it. They could cancel the whole show or find someone else to play leading lady. She wasn't going to give up this wonderful chance for a silly little amateur play!

They would have to cancel the whole show of course. It had taken Delia weeks to learn the part so it wasn't likely that anyone could learn it in a day. But as a matter of fact Delia didn't think about it much—her thoughts and dreams had flown before her to South Africa—and when by chance she did happen to think about it she decided that there was no need to consider Freddie's feelings . . . Freddie hadn't considered *her* feelings, had he?

Eulalie was in a different category. Delia wished she had been able to go and say good-bye, but that was impossible. For one thing there had been no time and for another she could not say good-bye to Eulalie without revealing her plans. Eulalie would be angry—every bit as angry as Freddie—and Delia simply could not face it. She was slightly in awe of Eulalie.

Delia comforted herself with the thought that she would write a very nice letter to Eulalie and explain everything—explain that here was her chance of 'seeing a bit of the world'. These were Eulalie's own words; she had said, 'You ought to see a bit of the world'. Delia was taking her advice so she could not complain, could she?

"What are you thinking about, Delia?" asked Esther.

"I was thinking about Eulalie. I wish I could have gone and said good-bye to her but there wasn't time."

"There wasn't time for anything," Esther declared. "We've been rushing about so madly that I've lost all idea of time.

I can scarcely believe that Walter's luncheon-party at The Owl was only yesterday."

CHAPTER NINETEEN

THE long spell of warm sunny weather had changed the eating habits of many of the inhabitants of the British Isles but not those of the Bloggses (they continued to have hot meals at the usual hour); so when Daphne and Flo returned home, after helping the Palmers to clear up the debris of the luncheon-party at The Owl and to give the place 'a bit of a redd up' as requested, they found their parents sitting down to a fine large meal of sausages and mash and baked beans. The sausages were done to a turn, golden brown in colour, the mash was as white as snow.

"Ooh, my fav'rite supper!" exclaimed Daphne.

Mrs. Bloggs knew this already—naturally she knew the tastes of each member of her family—so she merely nodded and smiled.

For a time the jaws of the Bloggses were fully occupied in mastication but when their appetites had been satisfied they began to talk. Mrs. Bloggs had been waiting eagerly for this moment, she wanted to hear all about the party. Fortunately the Bloggs sisters had been in different departments—so to speak—Daphne could provide information about what had taken place in the kitchen and Flo could describe the costumes of the guests.

"Mrs. Palmer cooked it all 'erself. She was a cook before she married Mr. Palmer," declared Daphne. "The soup was cold—she 'ad it ready in the fridge—looked like cold tea with little bits of vedge floating on the top."

"Mr. Musgrave mixed the drinks," said Flo. "There was a whole lot of bottles—'e mixed them together and stirred them up in a big glass jug with ice and 'e gave me and Vi a glass to taste before the guests arrived. Very nice and free, Mr. Musgrave is . . . funny taste it 'ad," she added thoughtfully.

"She mashed the pertaters," said Daphne. "Then she rolled it in balls and fried them—"

"Miss Delia wore 'er blue with the white collar and cuffs."

"Leg o' lamb—crisp and brown with brown gravy. Mum couldn't 'ave cooked it nicer . . ."

"Mrs. Musgrave 'ad a new dress—ever so nice she looked—and a white 'at and gloves. She came before the others and Mr. Musgrave and 'er were talking together when I took in the rolls—talking very earnest about something; very quiet. Then Mrs. Musgrave sed, 'Thursday is impossible' and Mr. Musgrave laughs and ses, 'Nothing is impossible'. That was all I 'eard."

This was much more interesting to Mrs. Bloggs than iced soup and leg of lamb with brown gravy. She pursued the subject up hill and down dale, offering all sorts of wild suggestions as to why Thursday should be impossible—and impossible for what—until even Flo who had put up the hare became wearied with the chase.

"Miss Rose was all in pink," said Flo. "She wears pink dresses all the time. She's got a nice blue one but she doesn't never put it on—'angs in 'er cupboard, that's all—'er name is Rose," added Flo somewhat unnecessarily.

"P'raps she's got a boy," suggested Daphne thoughtfully. "I mean when Vi was going with that feller in Ernleigh and the feller sed 'e liked 'er in blue she never wore nothing else for weeks. She gave me a pink dress she 'ad and then she wanted it back when the feller took up with someone else."

The Bloggs family had listened to this tragic tale before—more often than they wanted—so they were unmoved.

"Miss Rose couldn't 'ave got a boy," declared Mrs. Bloggs. "She ain't been 'ome more than a month—"

"It's my belief she 'as," said Flo.

"You don't say!" cried Mrs. Bloggs. "She 'asn't wasted 'er time!"

"Miss Delia'll be on the shelf, proper!" exclaimed Daphne giggling delightedly.

"Now don't you say nothing," Flo warned them—somewhat alarmed at the excitement her news had aroused. "All I sed was, 'it's my belief'—and that's all it is."

"Well, go on, Flo," urged Mrs. Bloggs. "You musta 'eard something—"

"I didn't 'ear nothing. I don't listen at key-'oles like some people. Like Vi Danks," she added hastily (in case Daphne should think the cap was intended for *her*). "Vi couldn't 'ave known all that about the Blakes 'aving rows if she 'adn't 'ad 'er ear glued to the key-'ole."

"People shouts when they 'as rows," Mr. Bloggs put in. He was not quite such a talker as the female members of the family but although he pretended to a certain male superiority he usually followed the conversation with interest and made an occasional pithy remark.

"Well, go on, do," said Daphne to her sister. "You got to be prodded like Joe Waters's donkey. If you didn't 'ear nothing what did you see?"

Thus encouraged Flo revealed the fact that Miss Rose went up to the Abbey Woods every afternoon. She put on a nice clean dress and went on winged feet. (As Flo put it, 'She looked like as if she was off to meet a boy'.) She took her paints and pencils and a painting-book and was away for hours and hours. Sometimes she returned for tea but more often she did not.

"That's not much," declared Mr. Bloggs who was inclined to pooh-pooh Flo's story. "It takes a long time to paint pictures. Now if you'd seen that there book—"

"That's just what I did! The book was on 'er dressing-table this very morning when I did 'er room so I took a glance through it. I wouldn't never read letters," declared Flo virtuously, "not unless they was torn up careless-like and dropped in the W.P.B. but pictures is different. There ain't nothing private about pictures."

Her family agreed with these principles.

"What kind of pictures?" they wanted to know.

"Pictures of the Abbey—ever so nice, they were—and there was two pictures of a boy, a young feller with curly 'air and a squint."

"A squint!" exclaimed Mrs. Bloggs in dismay.

Flo nodded. "And there was a picture of Miss Rose—I knowed it was 'er, 'cos of the pink dress and the buttons down the front. Very good, it was."

"Done by 'im!" cried Daphne breathlessly. "Done by the feller with the squint!"

"You're going too fast," said Mr. Bloggs. "It's all those movies you go to that makes you think things like that. If that's all you knows, you don't know nothing. The feller with the squint mighta been anyone. It don't mean she met 'im in the woods."

For a moment Flo was flummoxed, but only for a moment. "But 'e was sitting on the stones!" she cried triumphantly. "Sitting on a bit of the wall with a blue shirt and a loverly crease in 'is trousers—'e looked for all the world like a film star!"

"I never seen a film star with a squint," declared Mr. Bloggs, opening the evening paper and turning to the sports news to see if by any chance Dancing Lady had won the three-thirty. Unfortunately Dancing Lady had not, but as Mr. Bloggs had only risked a bob each way he was not unduly depressed.

Mr. Bloggs had said the last word on the subject, for none of his family had ever seen a film star with a squint, but afterwards when Flo and Daphne were undressing for bed it dawned upon Flo that her father's argument was beside the point.

"I never sed 'e was a film star," she explained to her sister. "I never thought it reelly; it was just the crease in 'is trousers and the posh blue shirt . . . but that don't mean she ain't meeting 'im on the sly and carrying on with 'im."

Daphne nodded thoughtfully, but did not speak. She was trying to think of a young man in Shepherdsford who would fill the bill, but she could think of none except Joe Waters, the owner of the reluctant donkey. Joe certainly had a formidable squint but could not be imagined with a posh blue shirt and a lovely crease in his trousers.

"We better ask Mum," said Daphne yawning.

CHAPTER TWENTY

1

MRS. Bloggs often said that Puggy had more sense than many a Christian. She talked to him when her family were out at work and especially when she had a problem on her mind. On this particular afternoon (it was Monday, and therefore washing day) Mrs. Bloggs had a big problem on her mind. For although she was a gas-bag and enjoyed a bit of gossip, she was a kind-hearted, motherly woman with a good deal of common sense.

"It's like this, Puggy," explained Mrs. Bloggs. "I've got two girls of my own—and if I was to 'ear that Daph or Flo was meeting a feller in the Abbey Woods I'd 'ave to do something about it. Specially a young feller with a squint. There's something about a squint that puts me off. You might say 'e can't 'elp it—and you'd be right—but all the same . . ."

She sighed and plunged another batch of linen into the tub. She had been washing all morning but the warm weather had increased her intake considerably so she had not yet finished her work.

"Well, that young girl ain't my basket of trouble, and you might say it ain't none of my business who she meets or what she does, but she's a young girl the same as Daph and Flo. Girls is girls, Puggy."

Hearing his name, Puggy wagged his tail.

"More sense than many a Christian," said Mrs. Bloggs fondly.

"I'd go to 'er mum," continued Mrs. Bloggs after a short silence. "But some'ow I don't see myself going to 'er mum and splitting on 'er. 'Sides, what do I know? I don't know nothing for certain. It's all just guesses—might be all moonshine—and 'er mum would want to know what I'd 'eard and who told me; like as not Flo would get the sack! So that's out, Puggy."

Again Puggy agreed.

"Well, I dunno," said Mrs. Bloggs thoughtfully. "A rare problem—that's what it is. I've got to know for certain sure before I can do much about it. Looks as if I'll 'ave to do a bit of sleuthing on my own. Looks as if you and me'll 'ave to go walkies."

At this magic word Puggy immediately began to bark and leap about in a frenzied manner quite unbecoming to his years and weight.

"Oh yes, I dessay you're pleased," agreed Mrs. Bloggs reluctantly. "It's all very nice for you that's got four good legs and no bunions! But all the same there's nothing else for it that I can see. I could leave it alone and 'ope for the best but I'll 'ave it on my mind till I've done something." She squeezed the soapsuds off her hands and removed her apron.

The afternoon was extremely warm and Mrs. Bloggs was aware that it was a steep uphill climb to the Abbey Woods, but it was quite unthinkable to go out without wearing the correct outdoor apparel of coat and hat and gloves—she would as soon have thought of going out in her nightdress.

It took her half an hour to prepare for the expedition, and Puggy watched her anxiously all the time, but at last she was ready (the mirror showed her short stout figure attired in a brown cloth coat with a fur collar and a brown felt hat) and having shut all the windows, locked the door and slipped the key under the mat, Mrs. Bloggs set forth to the Abbey Woods.

2

Shepherdsford was deserted, for it was now three o'clock—the hottest time of the day—and everyone who was able to rest was resting.

Mrs. Bloggs passed through the village unseen and began toiling up the hill. Her face became redder every minute. Puggy frisked like a lamb; sometimes he ran on in front and sat down on the path and looked back, panting, his tongue hanging out of his mouth like a bright red rag; sometimes he lagged behind, beguiled by delicious smells; sometimes he darted into the bushes to chase a non-existent rabbit.

It was seldom that Puggy was taken for such enjoyable 'walkies'. Mr. Bloggs always exercised him after tea and one of the girls took him for a run before bed-time, but that was routine. This 'walkies' was unexpected and therefore all the more delightful—and his companion gave him absolute freedom. Indeed his companion was too obsessed with her own discomfort to bother much about Puggy, she was extremely hot and her feet had begun to hurt almost unbearably. Several times she almost abandoned her project ... but then she remembered Daph and Flo. This girl, Rose Musgrave, was unknown to Mrs. Bloggs but she was a girl— just like Daph and Flo, and probably just as silly. (Supposing it was Flo thought Mrs. Bloggs. I wouldn't put it past Flo to be'ave silly, nor Daph neither if it comes to that. Girls is girls when there's a man to lead them into mischief). She sighed heavily and toiled on.

When she reached the Abbey Woods Mrs. Bloggs called Puggy and put him on the lead.

"Seems a shame," she admitted. "But we'll 'ave to go cautious, you and me. We're sleuthing—like that there man on the telly."

It was cooler beneath the trees but the path was even rougher; the roots of the great oaks straggled across it like serpents. Mrs. Bloggs was not used to rough paths so she stumbled frequently. She and Puggy were silent; partly because Mrs. Bloggs was breathless but more because she was frightened. The silence in the woods seemed unnatural ... and it was unfortunate that quite suddenly she remembered the Black Friar. Once or twice she thought she saw him out of the corner of her eye lurking amongst the trees, but when she looked at him properly he had vanished.

"Gives me the willies," she whispered to her companion. "Wouldn't come 'ere at night if you was to give me a 'undred pounds."

Quite unexpectedly she emerged from the shade of the trees and saw before her the ruins of the Abbey (thick ruined walls and heaps of broken stones) and here she hesitated, blinking her eyes, half blinded by the sunshine. There was nobody to be seen, but that did not mean there was nobody here. Picking her way carefully amongst the rubble and the tall nettles and patches of willow herb, Mrs. Bloggs began her search. Soon she was rewarded by the sounds of voices.

The sounds came from behind a broken pillar which had once formed part of an archway leading into the Great Hall. Again Mrs. Bloggs hesitated but only for a moment. Her heart was beating very fast as she went round the corner.

There they were! A young girl in a pink gingham frock sitting upon a block of stone and a man in pale grey trousers lying upon the sun-bleached turf. They were not very close to each other and they were just talking—that was all. Mrs. Bloggs had been afraid . . . well, she didn't quite know what she had been afraid of.

A stone rattled beneath her foot and they both looked round, startled. The man sat up and she saw him properly and recognised him at once. It was Mr. Edward Steyne.

"Good afternoon," said Mrs. Bloggs somewhat breathlessly.

They both replied to her greeting politely.

"Very warm, isn't it?" said Mrs. Bloggs, putting on her best party manner. She added, "I'm just taking Puggy for a walk."

Puggy barked and pulled at the lead so his mistress let him go and he frolicked up to his new friends. He was a sociable animal.

"What a nice little dog!" exclaimed the girl as she bent down and fondled him.

She was as pretty as a picture, decided Mrs. Bloggs; far too pretty to be meeting a man in a deserted wood—and far too young. Scarcely more than a child! And, according to Daph, Mr. Edward Steyne was not all he should be! Still he was Mr. Edward Steyne, Lady Steyne's stepson.

In a way Mrs. Bloggs was relieved that it was he and no other, but she did not know what to do.

"I dessay you don't know me, Mr. Steyne," she said. "I'm Mrs. Bloggs."

"Mrs. Bloggs?" echoed Edward in bewilderment.

"I'm Daph's mother," she explained. He still looked bewildered so she added, "Daph that works at Underwoods. I'm 'er mother."

"Oh, I see," said Edward. "Yes, of course . . . and you're taking your dog for a walk. Yes, of course. How nice!"

There was a short but somewhat uncomfortable silence. Mrs. Bloggs had time to notice the sketch-book and the open box of paints (she wished she could ask to see the pictures in that book but it would have taken much more effrontery than she possessed). She had time to wonder about the squint; Mr. Steyne had no squint (Flo had been wrong about that) but all the same his eyes were not—exactly—what you might call—honest. His eyes did not meet the eyes of Mrs. Bloggs fairly and squarely. (Knows 'e's doing what 'e didn't ought, decided Mrs. Bloggs). But there was nothing she could do about it; she realised that.

"Oh well," she said. "Me and Puggy 'ad better be off. Time I was going 'ome to get the tea." She called Puggy and put him on the lead and off she went.

She was late of course. The others were having tea when she went in.

"Well I never!" exclaimed Daphne.

"We thought you was lost!" cried Flo.

"Wot 'ave you been up to, Mimer?" demanded her husband.

Mrs. Bloggs took off her coat and hat, she also removed her shoes which were giving her severe pain.

"Puggy and me went walkies," she told them.

"You look 'ot," declared her husband.

"I ain't 'alf 'ot. I'm just about roasted."

"Well, what d'you expect on a roasting afternoon?"

Mrs. Bloggs did not answer the question. She said, "Pour me out a cuppa, Flo. I'm just about all in."

"You been up to something, Mimer," declared Mr. Bloggs suspiciously.

"That's right. I been up to the Abbey Woods."

Her family gazed at her, open-mouthed with astonishment.

"Why not?" she demanded, sipping the mustard-like brew with relish. "Anyone as likes can take a walk up to the Abbey. There's no law against it as I knows of. Puggy and me took a walk up to the Abbey to see if anyone was there."

"And was there?" asked Flo eagerly.

Mrs. Bloggs nodded.

"You mean you saw them?"

"I saw them—*and* talked to them," said Mrs. Bloggs.

Her family was struck dumb.

"Give me another lump, Flo," said Mrs. Bloggs. "Seems I want a bit more sugar—I don't want nothing to eat. Yes, I saw them *and* talked to them. It was Miss Rose Musgrave and Mr. Edward Steyne—that's who it was. There was paints and things lying about. You was wrong, Flo, Mr. Edward ain't got no squint but it was 'im all the same. They was sitting talking, so I just sed good afternoon and I was taking Puggy a walk and—"

"You didn't ought to 'ave done it, Mimer," interrupted Mr. Bloggs in alarm.

"Well, I'm glad I done it," declared Mrs. Bloggs defiantly.

"I told you Mr. Edward was shifty," began Daphne in excitement. "I told you 'e wasn't no good, and you see—"

"Now listen!" exclaimed her father. "Just you listen to me. All this ain't got nothing to do with us. There's to be no talk about it, see?"

"But, Dad—" began Flo.

"You 'old your tongue, Flo."

"But, Dad, I could give 'er a 'int—just a 'int, that's all. That couldn't do no 'arm. She didn't ought to be carrying on that way. I mean she's nice—Miss Rose is."

"You 'old your tongue, Flo!" exclaimed Mr. Bloggs in a louder tone than before.

"But, Dad, she's just a kid—"

"Did you 'ear what I sed, Flo?"

Flo relapsed into silence.

"Now then, you listen to me, all of you," shouted Mr. Bloggs, working himself up and hitting the table with his clenched fist. "You'll—'old—your—tongues. I don't want no trouble in this fam'ly—nor no scandal neither—nor no tale-bearing. Mr. Edward Steyne is Mr. Edward Steyne—see? Mum didn't ought to 'ave put 'er nose into it, but she's done it so it can't be 'elped—"

"There's no law against it, as I knows of—just passing the time of day—"

"There's a law against scandal," declared Mr. Bloggs frowning in a threatening manner. "And if any of you ses a word about it scandal is what there'll be."

His family gazed at him in alarm.

"You'll go to prison, that's what'll 'appen."

"Prison!" exclaimed Flo, aghast.

"That's what I sed—prison."

He looked round the table, wondering if he had said enough to ensure complete secrecy. Mr. Bloggs knew his family's propensity for gossip only too well!

"I just sed," began Mrs. Bloggs in a trembling voice—for of course she had not reported the whole conversation, "'Arry, I just sed—"

"We knows what you sed," declared her lord and master. "You told us what you sed. You didn't ought to 'ave gone and you didn't ought to 'ave sed nothing . . . but p'raps no 'arm will come of it if nobody ses nothing more. Mum's the word, see?"

They saw.

(All the same I'm glad I done it, thought Mrs. Bloggs. She's a young girl, just like Daph and Flo, and if 'e does the dirty on 'er I'll speak up, no matter what).

3

For some minutes after the departure of Mrs. Bloggs Edward and Rose were silent.

So that's the end of it, thought Edward. I had better make tracks before the storm blows up . . . before that wretched girl can say a word. If Amie hears about this she'll be furious. It would just about finish everything.

He was not really sorry that this was the end of it. Rose was a sweet little thing, her youth and innocence had attracted him at first and he had enjoyed talking to her and playing on her heart-strings, but now he was just beginning to feel slightly bored. Of course he had known all along that this was just an interlude—a dresden china idyll—delightful while it lasted but fleeting.

Edward decided he would leave early to-morrow morning, his sudden departure from Underwoods could easily be explained; he had only to say he had heard of a possible job. The prospect of returning to his small but extremely comfortable flat in Chelsea was distinctly pleasant.

Edward was brought back to earth by the sound of Rose's laughter.

"What a funny old thing!" said Rose. "She appeared so suddenly that I can scarcely believe she was real."

"She was real, all right—and it's no laughing matter."

"What do you mean?" asked Rose in surprise.

"She was a spy."

"A spy? What do you mean?"

"I mean just that. She was a spy. Somebody must have told her that we met here and she came to see if it was true."

"That funny old thing!" exclaimed Rose incredulously. "But she was quite nice—quite friendly—"

"Awfully nice and friendly. She's gone home to get the tea and tell her family that you and I are meeting daily in the Abbey Woods."

"But—but she was just out for a walk—to exercise her dog."

"That's nonsense. Do you think a woman like Mrs. Bloggs would toil up the hill—all that way in the blazing heat—just to exercise her dog? She isn't that sort of woman."

"How do you know?"

"By her clothes of course. You had only to look at her," declared Edward.

For a few moments Rose was silent. Then she said, "Oh well, it doesn't matter, does it? We aren't doing any harm. Anyone who likes can come up here to the woods, can't they?"

"You don't understand. It will be all round Shepherds-ford in half no time. Everyone in the place will be talking about us."

"Do you—think so—really?" asked Rose, filled with sudden unease.

"I know it," replied Edward with a mirthless laugh. "Every tongue in the place will be wagging. Amie is bound to hear about it—that woman's daughter works at Underwoods—and then the fat will be in the fire!"

Rose felt as if Edward had hit her in the face—it was so unlike the way he usually spoke that she could not have been more surprised if he had hit her. Quite suddenly she saw it all clearly; quite suddenly she was overwhelmed by a sense of guilt. She had drifted into these meetings with Edward so naturally, so gradually, that she had not realised the depths of her deceit. There had been a sort of magic in the whole affair; but now the magic was fading—and it looked—sordid.

"What are we to do?" she said in a whisper.

"Nothing at all. There's nothing to be done except say good-bye."

"You don't mean—good-bye? You don't mean—not see each other—any more?"

She looked at Edward, expecting comfort and reassurance, but Edward did not seem to be listening. He was gazing into the distance. Rose was not to know that already Edward was in London.

"I think—I'd better—go home," she said with a little catch in her breath.

Rose was half-way home, stumbling down the stony path unseeingly, when she suddenly remembered that The Bridle House was closed. Mummie was in London . . . with Delia.

Chapter Twenty-One

1

BERNARD returned home early that day. Monday was often a slack day at the office. He was about to hang his hat on the peg in the hall when he heard Meg singing gaily. He paused with his hand raised and listened. Yes, Meg was singing. She was in the kitchen—he could hear the clatter of dishes. She was washing up—and singing as she worked.

It was quite a long time since Bernard had heard Meg singing. There had been a cloud over her spirits—imperceptible to other people, perhaps, but palpable to Bernard. Did this mean that the cloud had passed and Meg was feeling better? He wondered if he should go in and speak to her or whether it would be wiser to take no notice and leave her alone. Then he discovered that his feet were taking him straight into the kitchen.

"Hallo, Meg!" he said. "I'm home early."

She turned from the sink and smiled at him—and she looked so adorable with her curls in disorder and her eyes shining that he was obliged to kiss her.

Margaret put her arms loosely round his neck and looked up at him. "I'm happy," she said.

"Yes, I heard you singing. I'm glad you're happy, darling."

"Oh Bunny, how lucky I am!"

"I'm glad," he repeated.

"I'm terribly lucky. I don't deserve it. I've got everything I want. There aren't many people who can say that, are there?"

"I can say it. I got everything I wanted when I got you."

She hesitated for a moment and then she said, "Yes, of course—that's the important thing—to have each other. I suppose I was ungrateful to want more."

"You wanted more?"

"Just one more thing, that's all, and now—"

"Now you've got it?"

"I'm going to get it," she told him, half laughing and half serious. "Oh Bunny, can't you guess?"

Of course he ought to have guessed—he was not usually so dense—but he couldn't.

"Oh Bunny!" cried Meg. "Oh Bunny, you are a silly old thing, aren't you? It's a baby of course."

"A baby!"

"Yes of course," said Meg. She was really laughing now—laughing at the astonishment writ large upon her husband's face. "Oh Bunny, people do quite often get babies when they're married. Didn't you know? Didn't your mother tell you about it when you were little? They go out together when the moon is full and find a real live baby under a gooseberry bush!"

"Oh Meg!"

"It's true," she told him. "It's really and truly true. I've got everything now—everything I want. I'm the happiest woman in the whole wide world. It's quite—it's quite frightening to be as happy as me."

"Oh Meg—and I never knew—if only you'd told me—"

"What was the good of telling you?" asked Meg, opening her eyes very wide.

(No, it wouldn't have been much *good*, reflected Bernard as he wheeled the tea-trolley into the sitting-room. It wouldn't have been much good—but it would have saved me a lot of worry).

They sat together upon the sofa to have their tea. Bernard was obliged to drink his tea with his left hand; his right was otherwise engaged.

"We must have the spare-room done up," said Margaret dreamily. "All white, I think, with white furniture."

"Rose-pink curtains," suggested Bernard.

"White with blue forget-me-nots—and a blue carpet."

Bernard readjusted his ideas. "Yes, of course," he agreed. "We'll call him Bernard, won't we?"

Bernard had thought of calling her Margaret—but he did not really mind. Meg was happy, that was all that mattered.

When Rose came in they disengaged themselves and sat up very slowly and reluctantly. As a matter of fact they had forgotten all about their guest.

"Hallo Rose! Have you had a nice walk?" asked Bernard kindly.

"I want Mummie!" exclaimed Rose bursting into tears.

2

Bernard had cleared away the tea-things and was washing up the cups and saucers when Margaret came downstairs.

"I don't know what on earth's the matter with her," declared Margaret. "She's all right now. I mean she stopped crying almost at once but she looks wretched. I've got her to go to bed."

"Shall we get the doctor?"

"She won't have the doctor. She says she's got a headache—that's all. I'm terribly worried about her, Bunny."

"You mustn't worry," said Bernard hastily. "It's very bad for you to worry."

"I know—but it's so unlike Rose. I wonder if she can have seen something in the woods and got a fright. Those woods are rather eerie. Perhaps she saw the Black Friar."

"The Black Friar?"

"Yes, the woods are supposed to be haunted by a Black Friar (quite a lot of people have seen him) and I remember when Rose was a child she was frightened of the Abbey Woods. We went up to the Abbey for picnics once or twice, but Rose had bad dreams after it and Mummie said I wasn't to take her again. Perhaps she saw the Black Friar this afternoon."

Bernard hesitated. He did not believe in the Black Friar, but perhaps she *had* seen something in the woods that had frightened her . . . a creature of flesh and blood!

In other words a man—a vagrant—that was possible. But he certainly was not going to mention this idea to Meg.

"It's probably a touch of the sun," he declared. "She goes about without a hat, doesn't she? The sun was blazing hot to-day—enough to give anyone a headache."

"Do you think I should ring up Mummie?"

"Does Rose want you to?"

"No, she doesn't. At first when I suggested it she said yes, and then, when she had calmed down a bit, she said no. She made me promise I wouldn't. She kept on saying it was just a headache and she was sorry she had been so silly."

"It was the sun," repeated Bernard. "I'm sure of it. If she isn't better in the morning we'll get the doctor. You mustn't worry, Meg. There's no need to worry. I'm sure she'll be better in the morning."

Bernard was always right, and this occasion was no exception to the rule. Rose appeared at breakfast looking a trifle wan but perfectly calm and composed. She agreed that her indisposition was due to the blazing hot sun and accepted the loan of a shady hat from her sister to go out into the garden. She also agreed that it had been foolish to walk up the steep hill to the woods and added that she would not go there again.

"Not in this heat," said Margaret.

"Not ever," declared Rose with unnecessary emphasis. Margaret was too wrapped up in her own secret happiness to notice the unnecessary emphasis, but Bernard noticed it and his suspicion was strengthened. He wondered if he ought to tell the Police of his suspicion that at there was a vagrant lurking in the woods. Supposing some other girl went up there alone! One never knew what might happen—the idea was too horrible to contemplate—but of course it was only a vague suspicion and obviously Rose did not intend to say a word about it . . . and to tell the truth Bernard did not relish the prospect of interviewing Sergeant Rambridge and asking that worthy man to take action upon a vague suspicion.

3

Rose had declared herself to be better, and this was true. At first there had been just misery in her heart. Her world lay in ruins; she wanted to be comforted and soothed; she wanted Mummie. But she was tired and had gone to sleep soon after Margaret had left her and a night's rest had worked wonders. She awoke early and leaned out of her bedroom window looking at the wide view and listening to the singing of the birds. Nobody could feel utterly and absolutely miserable on a lovely morning like this.

Kneeling here with her elbows on the window-sill Rose began to think about it properly; what a fool she had been! She had laughed at those girls at school who had 'gone all silly' about Mr. Logan, the drawing-master, but she was even sillier. She was wicked as well. She had told no lies, but she had acted lies; she had deceived her mother. What on earth had made her behave in such a horrible way? The answer was Edward had made her behave like that, he had cast a sort of spell upon her. He had made her believe he needed her friendship but he had not really valued it at all. She saw the illusion for what it was. Obviously the whole affair had meant nothing to him, it had just been a way of passing the idle afternoons . . . and then, when that woman appeared with her dog, he had been so taken up with his own fears as to what might happen that he had scarcely bothered to say good-bye. Every tongue in the place will be wagging. Amie is bound to hear about it . . . and then the fat will be in the fire!

Pride came to Rose's aid. The whole thing had meant nothing to Edward so she would make it mean nothing to her. She would *make* it mean nothing. The only reasonable and self-respecting thing to do was to wash it out and forget about it.

It was in this mood that Rose went down to breakfast, so of course she was only too ready to agree that her indisposition had been due to the blazing hot sun.

She spent the day in the garden with Meg, it was a good deal cooler; there were clouds in the sky, there was even a little shower in the afternoon . . . and that was distinctly pleasant. Meg did not seem to want to talk much, she was knitting a fine white shawl and could be heard murmuring the pattern to herself as she worked. Rose asked if it were for someone's baby and Meg smiled and said it was. Meg had dozens of school-friends and most of them were married and had babies—so Rose was not surprised.

When three o'clock struck, Rose thought of the Abbey Woods, for this was the hour she usually set forth upon her expedition, but curiously enough she felt nothing but a sense of relief, a sense of freedom. It was almost like a holiday. No more need to practise deceit; no more need to climb that steep path in the grilling sunshine; no more need to try to be 'grown-up' for Edward's benefit! She realised now that it had been a strain.

Rose snuggled down comfortably in Meg's comfortable chair and went on reading the book which she had discovered in Meg's bookcase.

"What are you reading?" asked Margaret. "Oh Rosie, what a baby you are! It's *The Wind in the Willows*! How often have you read it? You must know it by heart."

"Almost. That's why I like it," replied Rose smiling.

"You never showed me your sketches," said Margaret after a short silence.

"They weren't any good," replied Rose, looking up from her book.

"Mummie said they were very good. Do show me them, Rosie."

"I tore them up and burned them."

"Oh darling, why did you? Bunny said he would show them to a man—one of his clients who knows a lot about pictures. Why on earth did you burn them?"

"Because they weren't any good."

"But Rosie—"

"I can't draw," declared Rose. "I just did them for fun. You've either got to be very good at a thing or else leave it alone. It's the same with anything," she added. "I mean look at all the time Delia wasted practising music and now she never plays at all."

"Oh, Delia!" exclaimed Margaret scornfully. "That was different."

"I think it's the same—really. It's no use doing anything unless you can do it well. I'm going to study French instead."

Margaret was about to pursue the subject further but she saw that Rose had snuggled deeper into her chair and was engrossed in her book . . . so she said no more. Perhaps it was just as well, thought Margaret. Amateur water-colours were awful unless they were really good; French would be much more useful.

Bernard did not come home to lunch, but he returned for supper and was regaled with his favourite supper-dish—

Swedish Fish Pie (which consists of a pastry flan filled with a mixture of fish and cheese and tomatoes). Margaret made it and Rose watched her carefully. Rose had decided to study French but cooking was useful too and Meg was well worth watching.

"I love cooking," she explained as she flaked the fish and rolled out the pastry.

"It's your Thing," said Rose.

"Well, perhaps," agreed Margaret. "It isn't a very ambitious Thing, but it's useful. You've got to be a little bit greedy to be a good cook—I mean you've got to appreciate good food yourself—but even if I didn't like cooking very much I would enjoy cooking for Bunny."

"Because he appreciates good food or because you love him?"

"Both—you little goose!" replied Margaret laughing.

Chapter Twenty-Two

1

Tuesday had been cooler but Wednesday was as hot as ever. From all parts of the country came news of water-shortage and warnings to use the precious fluid as sparingly as possible; to take fewer baths and to make quite certain that there were no leaking taps in the house.

Eulalie Winter curtailed her ablutions with reluctance—she liked two baths a day—but on the other hand she enjoyed the warm sunshine and you couldn't have everything in this imperfect world. She was lying in her hammock beneath the tree when Freddie appeared. It was unusual for him to visit her at this hour in the morning, not only because he had his work to do but also because of the ban of secrecy which they had imposed upon themselves. Still she was not really surprised to see him.

"So you've heard!" she exclaimed.

"Oh yes, I've heard," said Freddie. He kissed her lightly and flung himself down on the grass beside her. "I've just had a letter. I felt as if the skies were falling when I read it."

"It's sickening," she agreed. "I rang up the clubhouse about twenty minutes ago to tell you the glad news but you were out. Cynthia told me about it when she came this morning."

"Who the heck is Cynthia?"

"Oh, you know, darling. You've often heard me natter about Cynthia. She's my daily and she's a friend of Daphne Bloggs who 'obliges' at Underwoods, see?"

Freddie tried to work this out. "No, I don't get it," he declared.

"Oh Freddie, you aren't usually so dense!" said Eulalie laughing a little and patting his shoulder to show that this was not meant unkindly. "Daphne saw Edward going off to London, bag and baggage, and she told Cynthia and Cynthia told me. What could be simpler?"

"You mean Edward has gone!" exclaimed Freddie aghast.

"I thought you knew! I mean I thought that was what—"

"Dear me, no," said Freddie with bitter satire. "I merely heard that Delia had gone, that's all . . . dress rehearsal to-night with no Ralph and no Angela! How jolly!"

"Delia has gone! What do you mean?"

"I had a charming little note from her this morning, written from London. She's *so* sorry to leave us in the lurch but she's going to the Cape with her stepbrother and she's *terribly* busy buying clothes. It has all happened in such a hurry—and she's mine, with love."

"I can't believe it!" cried Eulalie sitting bolt upright in astonishment.

"Isn't she a little swine! She was mad keen to get that part—Helen could have done it much better—and now, at the eleventh hour, off she goes!" He paused and then added, in a different tone, "Oh well, I suppose this is where we start cancelling the whole show."

"To the Cape—with Walter!" exclaimed Eulalie, whose mind was still taken up with this incredible fact. "I just simply can't believe it. She never said a word to me. In fact the last time I saw her she could talk of nothing but the play."

"When was that?"

"Oh, several days ago. It must have been Saturday. Yes, I haven't seen her since then."

"I thought you saw her nearly every day."

"Yes," admitted Eulalie. "Yes, she usually dropped in to see me in the afternoon. It does seem a little odd now that you mention it . . . but somehow I never noticed. My mind was taken up with something else." She blew a little kiss to Freddie but he was too dejected to respond.

"How do we start cancelling the show?" he asked gloomily. "Where do we begin? This'll just about wreck the club: halls, scenery and the hire of costumes to pay for and not a cent on the credit side . . . tickets to be returned! It wouldn't be quite so bad if we were just giving the play in Shepherdsford, but we're supposed to be putting it on at Ernleigh—on Saturday night! Oh gosh, why did I let them persuade me to do it? I had a feeling from the beginning that something would go wrong."

"Nothing has gone wrong."

"Nothing—wrong!" he exclaimed. "The whole show has got to be cancelled—"

"Need we cancel the show?"

"Need we cancel the show!" echoed Freddie. "I suppose we put on the play without Angela and Ralph? Is that what you mean?"

"You could play Ralph quite easily; you know the whole thing."

"I suppose I could—at a pinch—but that isn't much use. Nobody could mug up the part of Angela at a moment's notice. Who's going to step in and play Angela—tell me that."

"I am," said Eulalie simply.

He looked at her incredulously.

"Oh Freddie—your face!" cried Eulalie, laughing. "I'm going to play Angela—see?"

"But, my dear girl, how could you possibly mug it up in time? That unspeakable young woman chatters like a magpie all the way through. Do you realise the dress rehearsal is to-night and the play is supposed to be taking place to-morrow?"

"It *will* take place to-morrow. Oh Freddie, this is fun! I'm so glad Ralph and Angela have eloped! Don't look at me like that; I shall die of laughing!"

Freddie did not laugh. He said, "Nobody could do it. Honestly—"

"I could," she told him. "I know Angela from A to Z. I've been coaching Delia for weeks—and believe me it was pretty hard going. I've been dinning it into her; dinning and dinning until I was nearly crazy."

Freddie looked at her. Quite literally he was struck dumb.

"It's true," she declared. "I could step into the part now, this very minute, without the slightest trouble—and what's more I will."

"Eulalie, do you mean it?"

"Yes, of course. I've told you I know every word . . . and fortunately the costume is here. We arranged for it to come here so that she could try it on this morning. It may need some slight alterations but I can easily manage that."

"It's too good to be true! Why on earth did you take so much trouble with the girl?"

"I don't know," said Eulalie thoughtfully. "I don't know why I bothered. I don't pretend to be altruistic (sometimes when she was particularly dense I nearly gave up the struggle in despair) but I like Delia, you know. I told you that before—"

"You can have her!" Freddie exclaimed.

"Brother Walter is having her," Eulalie reminded him. "I haven't met Brother Walter, of course, but from what I've heard about him he's a pretty tough nut. He won't stand any nonsense. It will do our Delia a lot of good to be taken in hand by a man."

"Do you really think you could do it?" asked Freddie, who was more interested in the production of *The Mulberry Coach* than in Walter Musgrave's affairs.

"Try me," suggested Eulalie.

They went into the house together, to the music room.

2

It was obvious to Freddie after the first five minutes that Eulalie had spoken no more than the truth when she had said she 'could step into the part now, without the slightest trouble' . . . and of course she was ten times better than Delia, for she had ten times more 'pep'. She was especially good in the scene at the inn when Ralph and Angela crept in furtively hand-in-hand and embraced with ardour. Freddie was good at that, too—ever so much better than Mark or Edward.

"Goodness, Freddie!" exclaimed Eulalie when she had emerged from the ardent embrace. "You're not going to do that 'on the night' I hope."

"I'll wait till next week—in London," said Freddie laughing.

"You've booked the rooms and everything?" she asked.

"All fixed," he replied. He hesitated and then added, "You realise, don't you, that I haven't got a penny to my name except the miserable pittance I get from the Golf Club."

"That's all right. I'm not rolling, but I have enough pennies for two . . . but we don't want to stay in Shepherdsford for the rest of our lives. I think we could make money, you and I, and enjoy ourselves into the bargain."

"I'm all for adventure! You've got some scheme. I can see it in your eyes."

Eulalie laughed. "What about running a hotel on the Riviera?"

"There are dozens of hotels already."

"Dozens of luxurious expensive hotels but not many of the other kind."

"A cheap hotel!" he exclaimed in dismay.

"Not exactly cheap. I was thinking of a moderate one. The sort of place for people who want to travel and see other countries—like Aggie."

"Aggie who?" asked Freddie in bewilderment. Then he said "Oh, of course. I'd forgotten about Aggie. Sorry!"

Eulalie was not sorry he had forgotten about Aggie. It showed that she was not haunting him (which was what Eulalie had feared). She said, "I never thanked you for listening to that sordid story, Freddie. It was kind of you . . . and I want to tell you that I feel much happier about it now. They say confession is good for the soul, don't they? Well, anyhow, my confession has done me good. I don't feel bitter about Aggie any more. She had that frightful urge to travel and see the world. It was a positive mania."

"So you want to run a hotel for Aggies?"

"I think one could make money out of it too," said Eulalie frankly. "If we once got started we could have a chain of hotels in different places—if you see what I mean."

"Pass on the Aggies from one to another. Yes, I believe you've got something there," agreed Freddie thoughtfully.

"It's just an idea," she declared. "We can think about it later. The first thing to think about is the dress rehearsal."

"Let's have a joke with them," suggested Freddie smiling. "Listen, Eulalie . . ."

CHAPTER TWENTY-THREE

1

SHEPHERDSFORD Village Hall was bare and bleak when the members of the Dramatic Club began to arrive for the dress rehearsal. They drifted in one by one and stood about in little groups talking in low voices. The big empty hall was depressing.

"'All dressed up and no place to go!" said Tom Blake with an air of bravado. To tell the truth he felt a perfect fool in his velvet coat and knee breeches and his white wig. His white whiskers were in his pocket. He and Edna had had 'words' about them; she had wanted to glue them on to his face but he had refused to let her. He would have to wear them to-morrow night, but he was blowed if he would wear them for the dress rehearsal.

"It's eight," said Mark Henderson, glancing at his watch. "Where's Freddie, I wonder. He's usually up to time."

The other, looked round and took stock of their companions.

"Helen isn't here yet," said Sylvia in surprise.

"Where are Delia and Edward?" asked Edna.

Helen arrived at that moment. She was wearing a tweed coat and skirt.

"How funny you look!" exclaimed Helen hysterically. "You look as if you are going to act in a play!" They gazed at her, speechless with astonishment.

"Did you think there was going to be a play?" asked Helen. "Well, there isn't."

"What on earth do you mean?" demanded Tom Blake.

"Delia has gone, that's all. She's gone to London. She's ratted. She's left us high and dry. Just like her, isn't it?"

A babble of talk broke forth:

"Delia has gone? It can't be true!"

"I can't believe it! Delia was so keen—"

"Are you sure, Helen? Who told you?"

"Perhaps she's only gone for the day—"

"You don't seem to realise that the play is off!" cried Helen, raising her voice to make herself heard above the din. "You stand there talking nonsense! I've wasted hours learning that stupid old nurse's part and rehearsing it over and over again with Delia . . . and now she's walked out and left us in the lurch. If she had let us know a week ago I could have taken the part of Angela, but, oh no, she stuck to it like a leech! It's too late now—we're sunk. There won't be any play to-morrow night so you can all take off those ridiculous clothes and wash your faces and go home to bed."

It was at this moment that the door opened and Ralph and Angela appeared. (Their entrance was so beautifully timed that one might almost have supposed they had been listening for their cue at the key-hole). Ralph and Angela were attired in the correct costume and made up with consummate art.

"You seem a trifle surprised at our appearance," said 'Ralph'. This was a line from the play.

"Freddie!" exclaimed Mark. "It's you!—and Mrs. Winter!"

'Ralph' swept a low bow and 'Angela' sank in a graceful curtsey to the ground.

"I suppose this is a joke," said Helen coldly.

"It was meant to be," admitted Freddie. "But it seems to have fallen a bit flat."

"Mr. Stafford is being very naughty," explained Eulalie Winter, coming forward and resuming her normal manner. "He only heard this morning that Delia had gone away. At first we thought the play would have to be cancelled and then we decided that at all costs 'the play must go on'. So if you all agree I'll do my best to cope with Angela." She turned to Helen and smiled. "Of course if you would rather play Angela I'm quite willing to swap."

"I couldn't," said Helen frankly. "I've just been telling them. I could have done it a week ago. I can't now at the last minute."

"Can *she*?" murmured Edna Blake.

"Mrs. Winter is willing to try," said Freddie. "It's very kind of her to offer and I'm sure everyone will give her all the support they can. I should just like to point out that if we can't put on the play to-morrow night the Dramatic Club is finished."

"Finished?" echoed Helen incredulously.

"In other words, we're bust," declared Freddie. "We've been running the club on a shoe-string. We've spent a lot on this production. If we can't rake in some money we're done for. In fact I'm bound to tell you the club will be in the red and it will mean a whip-round."

There was a short silence. It was a silence of dismay.

"I think we ought to thank Mrs. Winter," said Mark. "It's very decent of her to—to say she'll—try."

There was a murmur of assent. Somebody started clapping. They all clapped—even Helen. She could not be the only person present not to clap and she disliked the idea of 'a whip-round' as much as anyone.

"Come on, then," said Freddie. "Let's start. Pull up your socks and do the best you can. Helen had better go and change. Look sharp, Helen."

"Edward isn't here yet," said Helen. "He comes on before I do, so there's no hurry—"

"He's gone away—went off yesterday morning. I'm taking his part. Hurry up, all of you, we don't want to be here all night."

They were so shattered that they made no comment upon Edward's departure . . . and of course this was a minor matter compared with the departure of Delia. Everyone was aware that Freddie could play Ralph without any difficulty. He had done so before.

2

The rehearsal was no worse than most dress rehearsals of amateur companies; in fact it was a good deal better, for all the actors had just received a severe shock. They had been plunged into Despair and had risen to Hope in the space of a few minutes. An experience such as this is liable to shake up the most phlegmatic temperament. So here they were, all keyed-up and on their toes.

There were hitches of course but nearly all the hitches were the fault of Eulalie who missed an occasional cue and required prompting and made quite a number of mistakes. She allowed herself to be helped out, murmuring apologies in a very charming manner. At first Freddie was worried (he was also surprised, for she had made no mistakes at all when they had run through the play that morning) and then, watching her carefully, he realised that the mistakes were deliberate—his future wife was even more clever than he had thought! Eulalie was acting a play of her own; it was a play within a play—a consummate piece of acting. Having thus decided Freddie cast care to the winds and enjoyed himself immensely; he entered into the play within the play.

"You missed a good many cues," he said with a worried frown.

"I just—stumbled through," said Eulalie humbly. "I couldn't have managed if everyone hadn't been so kind in covering up my stupid mistakes—"

"You were splendid," declared the other members of the cast.

"You made hardly any mistakes at all!"

"I don't know how you did it!"

"You were simply wonderful!"

(They did not know how wonderful she was.) Freddie's was the only voice that did not join in the paean of praise. "Oh, you weren't bad, considering," he admitted grudgingly. "But you'll have to do a good deal better if the play is to go on to-morrow night."

"Freddie you're crazy!" exclaimed Mark. "How can you possibly expect anyone to step into a part like that—"

"Of course the play can go on!" declared Tom Blake.

"Of course the play can go on!" echoed the others unanimously.

Sylvia threw her bonnet in the air and danced a little jig.

Chapter Twenty-Four

1

ESTHER and Delia spent two days in London buying clothes and other accessories for Delia's visit to the Cape. Delia seemed to thrive upon this arduous business; she was full of energy, her eyes shone like stars, even her hair seemed full of life. Indeed she was so unlike herself that Esther could scarcely believe that this girl was really her 'difficult Delia'.

"You're enjoying all this," said Esther with a sigh as they sat down for a few moments to eat a hasty meal.

Delia nodded. "I've always wanted to travel," she explained. "This is my Big Chance and I intend to make the most of it. I intend to enjoy every moment."

"I hope you'll get on with Walter. We don't really know very much about him."

"It will be all right," Delia declared. "It will be a worthwhile job to run Walter's bungalow—and Walter and I understand each other."

"You can always come home if you're unhappy—"

"Oh, of course, but I shan't be unhappy. It will be too marvellous for words."

Esther said no more. There was nothing more to say. Walter had business affairs in London, but he came to their hotel in the evening and had dinner and took Delia to a play. He wanted Esther to go too—he had taken a ticket for her—but Esther was tired, indeed she was absolutely exhausted, so she went to bed instead. It was hot in London, the air was sultry and the pavements were so baked by the sun that they burned her feet.

The second day of shopping was even hotter and more exhausting than the first and in the evening Walter took them to the Unicorn Restaurant and entertained them regally with a slap-up dinner and champagne. The Unicorn was 'all the rage' at the moment so it was thronged with fashionable people. In other circumstances Esther might have enjoyed it but to-night she was tired and dispirited so after dinner she went back to the hotel leaving Walter and Delia to dance. She got into bed and lay there with the window wide open listening to the constant roar of the traffic and thinking about this adventure of Delia's—this strange adventure into the unknown.

Esther had made up her mind to stop worrying about her family and of course it was useless to worry about Delia. Delia had made her own decision, she was determined to go and to 'enjoy every moment' and she was old enough to know her own mind. Apparently she had no regrets about leaving her home and her family—Esther was human enough to wish that Delia had shown just a little more feeling, but that was not Delia's way.

Even with the window wide open the hotel bedroom was hot and stuffy; Esther yearned for the sweet clean air of Shepherdsford and her own comfortable room. And suddenly she decided to go home to-morrow; there was no reason why she should not go straight home after seeing the travellers off at the airport. Why spend another miserable night in town?

There was a telephone beside her bed so she rang up Margaret then and there and announced her change of plan.

"Oh—yes—" said Margaret doubtfully. "The only thing is we've arranged to go to that play to-morrow night. Delia won't be in it of course, but Sylvia says it's going on just the same. Sylvia says it will be very good; Mrs. Winter is taking Delia's part."

"That will be all right," replied Esther. "I don't want you to meet me at the station. I can get a taxi."

"But what about Rose? We've got a ticket for Rose. We all intended to go together and come back here after the show. We're having a supper-party and we've asked several people. We thought it would be fun for Rose and cheer her up."

"Cheer her up?"

Margaret said hastily, "I just meant it would be fun for Rose to have a party, that's all. But she'll have to spend the night here. It would be too late for her to go home to The Bridle House after the party."

"There's no need for you to alter your arrangements."

"But Mummie, you would be there alone—or perhaps I could get Flo? I'm sure Flo would come and spend the night with you—"

"I don't want Flo," declared Esther. "I don't want anybody. All I want is to get home. Don't you understand?"

"Mummie, are you sure—"

"Yes, I'm sure. For goodness' sake don't fuss. I shall come by that train which arrives about seven and make myself some supper and go to bed early."

"It sounds rather dreary," said Margaret in a doubtful tone.

"It isn't in the least dreary," replied Esther firmly. "I'd far rather come home than spend another night in town. I've been alone before in The Bridle House and I didn't mind a bit."

"Well, if that's what you want—"

"Yes, that's what I want. You can get a loaf of bread and some milk for me—if it isn't a bother—and leave the key next door with the Braddocks."

"Yes, of course, but—"

"I don't know why you're fussing, Meg," said Esther a trifle irritably. "Just do as I say and don't fuss."

"All right," agreed Margaret . . . but she hesitated as she put back the receiver because somehow she felt a bit worried. Her mother was seldom irritable and seldom so firm and definite about her arrangements. Usually she was content to fall in with the arrangements of other people—to drift with the stream—however if that was the way Mummie wanted it there was nothing to be done except to carry out her instructions.

2

Esther's train was a little late; it was half past seven when her taxi drove up to The Bridle House. She was about to inquire next door for the key when she noticed that all the windows in the house were wide open and the front door ajar. For a moment she was alarmed . . . and then she decided that it could not be burglars. No unauthorised visitors would be such fools as to advertise their presence by opening all the front windows.

The taxi-driver carried her suitcase up the path, he dumped it in the hall and was paid and went away.

I'm home! thought Esther, standing there and enjoying the delightful feeling of peace and quiet and the familiarity of her own belongings. This was her own place—she would not have exchanged it for a palace—she felt as if she had been away for months.

Esther took off her 'London hat' and threw it on to the hall-table and went into the kitchen . . . and here she discovered her youngest daughter enveloped in a large blue apron stirring some concoction in a little saucepan on the electric stove.

"Rose!" exclaimed Esther in surprise.

"Oh Mummie!" cried Rose dropping the wooden spoon, rushing across the room and flinging herself into her mother's arms as if she had been a child of seven years old instead of a grown-up woman of seventeen.

"Rose! What's the matter?"

"Nothing—except I've missed you so frightfully. I shall never leave you—never—never—never—"

"No darling, of course not. Not for years and years—not until you're properly grown-up."

Esther had no idea what it all meant but apparently this was the right answer for she could feel Rose's whole body relax in her arms. She hesitated for a moment and then added, "But I thought you were going to the play?"

"I wanted to be here."

"Oh Rose, you shouldn't have given it up—and what about the party?"

"I didn't give it up. I mean it isn't 'giving up' if you do something you want to do more than the other thing, is it?"

"No, at least—"

"And I wanted to be here when you arrived. Darling Mummie, you don't mind, do you?"

"Mind? Of course not! It's lovely," declared Esther giving her a little gentle squeeze.

"You wouldn't rather be here alone?" asked Rose somewhat anxiously.

"No, of course not!"

"Meg said that was what you wanted—to be here alone. Meg was a little cross with me—just a tiny bit cross. She had arranged the party for me—but I couldn't help it. I wanted to be here. I wanted it more than anything. You understand, don't you?"

Esther said she understood (she didn't really understand but no doubt the lie was forgiven her). She had no idea what it was all about but she knew that for the last ten days or so there had been something wrong between herself and Rose;

there had been a sort of shadow, but now the shadow had vanished. She would have liked to know more about that shadow but she was much too wise to ask. Perhaps some-day Rose would tell her—and perhaps not.

For about a minute they stood there, looking at each other and smiling, and they were exactly the same height so they were looking straight into each other's eyes . . . and there was not the slightest vestige of a shadow.

Then suddenly Rose cried out in alarm, "Oh goodness, my pie!" and rushed to the oven.

"Your pie?"

"Yes, it's almost ready. I've got to brown it under the grill, that's all, so if you want to wash or anything you must be quick," said Rose earnestly. "It's a Swedish Fish Pie—Meg showed me—but somehow mine doesn't look quite the same as Meg's. I can't think why, because I did it exactly the same way . . ."

So Esther ran and washed away the grime of London as quickly as possible and in a very few minutes they were sitting at the kitchen table together eating Swedish Fish Pie—which certainly looked a little strange but tasted extremely good to Esther—and after that they had bread and honey and coffee.

It was a simple repast, not to be compared with the marvellous dinner of which Esther had partaken last night with Walter and Delia, but for all that Esther enjoyed it incomparably more. 'Better is a mess of pottage with love . . .' thought Esther as she held out her plate for another helping of Rose's Swedish Fish Pie.

There was a great deal to say; Rose wanted to hear all about Esther's adventures in London and Esther wanted the latest news of Meg and Bernard.

"They were kind to me—very kind," declared Rose. "But they don't really need anyone except each other and Meg was sort of vague. We sat in the garden most of the time. Meg didn't want to talk."

"Didn't want to talk!" exclaimed Esther in alarm. "Was she depressed and—and unhappy?"

"Not a bit. As a matter of fact she seemed happier than usual. She didn't want to talk because she was knitting a shawl in very fine wool and it was a difficult pattern. It was for somebody's baby."

"Whose baby?"

"I don't know. Meg has lots of friends and they all keep on having babies, don't they?"

Esther did not reply. A sudden thought had struck her . . . perhaps she ought to buy some fine white wool and look out that pattern for a baby's jacket which she had put away so carefully . . .

This delightful idea had taken Esther miles away, she returned to earth to hear Rose saying: "They'll be in the thick of it now."

"Who—what?" asked Esther in bewilderment.

"The play of course. If we want to see it we could go over to Ernleigh and see it on Saturday night."

"We will," said Esther nodding. "There's no reason why we shouldn't. It will be fun. We'll do all sorts of things together. You mustn't let me get into a rut. You could have a friend to stay—that would be nice, wouldn't it?—she could have Delia's room."

"I don't want anybody except you."

"Well—later, perhaps," said Esther. "One of your school-friends. I was thinking about it coming down in the train . . . and I was thinking you might like to join the Dramatic Club. You like acting, don't you?"

"Yes, I might do that," agreed Rose thoughtfully. "They asked me to join before but Delia wouldn't have liked it, would she?"

Esther did not reply to that. It was true, of course. Delia would not have liked it at all, but suddenly Esther realised that she and Rose had been planning a very happy life together—a life without Delia! They were planning to do all sorts of pleasant things which they could not have done if Delia were here . . . it seemed wrong, somehow; it seemed heartless.

"I expect you're glad to be home," said Rose after a short silence.

"Oh yes, indeed I am!" declared Esther. "It was baking hot in town and I got so tired and I was miserable about Delia."

"You needn't be miserable about Delia. She'll be perfectly happy. Delia has got what she wanted and Walter understands her. Walter will be able to manage her far better than we ever could. Honestly, Mummie, it will work out splendidly."

"I believe you're right!" exclaimed Esther, looking at her youngest daughter in surprise.

"And of course she may get married," added Rose.

"Get married!"

Rose nodded. "Walter has lots of friends—he said so—and one of them might want a wife. Delia is very pretty, isn't she? I don't suppose there are many pretty girls out there."

Esther could not help laughing a little at the air of gravity and wisdom with which Rose had spoken, but all the same she realised that such an eventuality was not impossible, it was not even very unlikely.

"Oh, you can laugh," said Rose smiling in sympathy. "Of course I may be wrong about that, but I just thought . . . and it would do Delia *such* a lot of good to get married and have lots and lots of children. She wouldn't have time to think so much about herself."

Esther was laughing heartily now. She said, "Oh well, we shall have to wait and see."

They had finished supper by this time so they washed up the dishes together and then went round the house to make sure that all the ground-floor windows were fastened, and they were in the hall on their way to bed when Rose paused and listened.

"Wait, Mummie!" she exclaimed. "What's that funny noise? A sort of rushing sound!" She threw open the front-door and added almost incredulously, "Yes, I thought it was! It's raining!"

It was raining quite hard, coming down from the cloudy sky in straight rods silvered by shafts of moonlight . . . and it was so long since they had seen real heavy rain that they stood at the door, arm in arm, for quite a long time and watched it without speaking.

A strange feeling of relief and happiness came to Esther and she realised how much the drought had strained her nerves. It was not exactly the water-shortage which had depressed her, nor the sight of the flowers in her beloved garden fading and drooping—though that was bad enough—it was something deep inside herself which had craved for rain. The drought had not lasted so very long (in comparison with foreign lands, rainless for months on end) but here, in England, neither the country nor the people are inured to prolonged periods of dry weather.

Now the tension was relieved . . . and not only the tension caused by the lack of rain but also the anxieties which Esther had suffered on behalf of her family. Delia had got what she wanted—something worthwhile to do; Meg was knitting a baby's shawl; and Rose, standing here beside her, had come through some strange experience and was once more Esther's very own.

It was all mixed up in Esther's mind. She only knew that all her worries had vanished and the roses in the garden would bloom again.

Meanwhile the rain continued to fall. Every leaf on every tree was dripping and there were drops of water like diamonds on the parched grass. The whole land seemed to be astir and a wet cool smell of wet cool earth, mingled with the scent of flowers, came drifting in through the open doorway.

"What a lovely smell!" said Rose softly. "It's the garden saying thank you."

Envoi

1

THE *Ernleigh Weekly Gazette* had a limited circulation and although it was read with avidity by people in the district who were interested in local affairs it was seldom to be met with outside the boundaries of the County. Occasionally however if something particularly exciting took place—such as a Dog Show or The Hunt Ball or a Charity Bazaar—there was an increased demand for the paper. The week following the production of *The Mulberry Coach* the issue was sold out with exceptional rapidity and two copies made extensive journeys by air-mail.

Delia Musgrave read her copy sitting on the veranda of Walter's bungalow on the Hallsey Estate and was surprised to learn that *The Mulberry Coach* had been produced in spite of her defection . . . but of course Eulalie was the obvious person to fill her shoes. Delia was just a trifle regretful that she had been unable to fill the shoes herself, however that could not be helped. To tell the truth Delia was not particularly interested in the account of the production, her surprise and regret were fleeting, for already Shepherdsford seemed far away and she was settling down and enjoying her new life almost as much as she had expected. She was enjoying the sunshine and the flowers and the feeling of importance engendered by her position; she was enjoying the attention and admiration of Walter's friends.

There were snags, of course. For instance Walter ordered her about rather more than she had expected, but she had sense enough to realise that Walter was the boss, so it was natural that he should be 'bossy' (if they were to live their life together she would have to toe the line) and although he was a little too fond of his own way he was appreciative of Delia's efforts to please him. Various innovations which she had suggested in the running of the bungalow had been accepted by Walter with approval and he was allowing her a free hand in redecorating the rooms and ordering new furniture from Cape Town.

"Order what you like," said Walter. "Go ahead and make it a comfortable home. At present it's just a place to live in."

So Delia went ahead and gradually the bungalow began to look more like 'a comfortable home' with rugs on the bare wooden floors, pretty curtains in the windows and vases of flowers on the tables. With all these important matters filling her mind it was no wonder that Delia's interest in *The Ernleigh Weekly Gazette* was only fleeting.

2

Another copy of *The Ernleigh Weekly Gazette* arrived by air-mail at a large, luxurious hotel in Cannes and was delivered to Mr. and Mrs. Frederick Stafford in their large, luxurious bedroom, the windows of which looked out over green gardens to the bright-blue waters of the Mediterranean Sea.

"Hallo, here's the *Gazette*!" exclaimed Mr. Stafford.

"The *Gazette*?" asked his wife in surprise. "D'you mean that funny little Ernleigh paper? Who on earth can have sent it, Freddie?"

"Well, as a matter of fact I asked Ernest to send it," replied Mr. Stafford. "I thought it would be rather fun to see what they said about us. I'll read it to you, shall I?" and without waiting for Mrs. Stafford's permission he proceeded to read out the notice in a solemn and portentous manner giving due emphasis to the flowery adjectives which the reporter had lavished upon *The Mulberry Coach*:

"On Saturday, at the Ernleigh Town Hall, there was a performance of *The Mulberry Coach* by the well-known author Jane Harcourt. It was given by the Shepherdsford Dramatic Club and provided a delightful evening's entertainment for a distinguished and appreciative audience. The play was a mixture of pathos, humour and tense excitement; the scenery and costumes were enchanting and the production went with a swing from start to finish in a manner seldom to be seen in the production of an amateur company."

"There, what d'you think of that, Mrs. Stafford?" asked Mr. Stafford pausing and looking up.

"Lovely," replied Mrs. Stafford giggling. "Simply gorgeous. Go on, Freddie. There's more, isn't there?"

"Lots more," he assured her. "'The best is yet to be!'"

"Mrs. Eulalie Winter looked charming in her crinoline gown of white muslin, sprigged with rosebuds, and acted her arduous role to perfection. Mr. Frederick

Stafford, as the gallant Ralph, supported her admirably—the love scenes were especially moving and convincing—and Mr. Ernest Lake gave a thoroughly satisfactory performance as Giles, the black-hearted villain of the piece. All the other characters were well represented, so much so that it is well-nigh impossible to pick out any one of them for special praise, but Miss Sylvia Newbigging as the innkeeper's daughter deserves mention for her sympathetic rendering of a difficult part. Her screams of fright when attacked by 'Giles' were almost too realistic.

"When the play ended there were innumerable curtain calls and large bouquets of fragrant blossoms were presented to the ladies of the company by ardent admirers; then 'Angela' appeared, led on by 'Ralph' and the two received vociferous applause. Mrs. Winter curtsied with consummate grace and Mr. Stafford, in a few well-chosen words, thanked the audience for the great welcome they had received that night and added that such an appreciative reception was most inspiring.

"The entertainment finished with an enthusiastic rendering of God Save the Queen in which everyone present took part.

"We understand that the Shepherdsford Dramatic Club produces a play annually and we can only hope we may have the pleasure of witnessing another production next year by this talented company."

Mr. and Mrs. Frederick Stafford were laughing so uncontrollably by this time that they were obliged to cling together for support.

THE END

AN AUTOBIOGRAPHICAL SKETCH
by D.E. Stevenson

EDINBURGH was my birthplace and I lived there until I was married in 1916. My father was the grandson of Robert Stevenson who designed the Bell Rock Lighthouse and also a great many other lighthouses and harbours and other notable engineering works. My father was a first cousin of Robert Louis Stevenson and they often played together when they were boys.

So it was that from my earliest days I heard a good deal about "Louis", and, like Oliver Twist, I was always asking for more, teasing my father and my aunts for stories about him. He must have been a strange child, a dreamy unpredictable creature with a curious fascination about him which his cousins felt but did not understand. How could ordinary healthy, noisy children understand that solitary, sensitive soul! And as they grew up they understood him even less for Louis was not of their world. He was born too late or too early. The narrow conventional ideas of mid-Victorian Edinburgh were anathema to him. Louis would have been happy in a romantic age, striding the world in cloak and doublet with a sword at his side, he would have sold his life dearly for a Lost Cause—he was ever on the side of the under-dog. He might have been happy in the world of today when every man is entitled to his own opinions and the Four Freedoms is the goal of Democracy.

My father was old-fashioned in his ideas so my sister and I were not sent to school but were brought up at home and educated by a governess. I was always very fond of reading and read everything I could get hold of including Scott, Dickens, Jane Austen and all sorts of boys' books by Jules Verne and Ballantyne and Henty.

When I was eight years old I began to write stories and poems myself. It was most exciting to discover that I could. At first my family was amused and interested in my efforts but very soon they became bored beyond measure and told me it must stop. They said it was ruining my handwriting and wasting my time. I argued with them. What was handwriting for, if not to write? "For writing letters when you're older," they said. But I could not stop. My head was full of stories and they got lost if I did not write them down, so I found a place in the box-room between two large black trunks with a skylight overhead and I made a little nest where I would not be disturbed. There I sat for hours—and wrote and wrote.

Our house was in a broad street in Edinburgh—45 Melville Street—and at the top of the street was St. Mary's Cathedral. The bells used to echo and re-echo down the man-made canyon. My sister and I used to sit on the window-seat in the nursery (which was at the top of the house) and look down at the people passing by. I told her stories about them. Some of the memories of my childhood can be found in my novel, *Listening Valley*, in which Louise and Antonia had much the same lonely childhood.

Every summer we went to North Berwick for several months and here we were more free to do as we wanted, to go out by ourselves and play on the shore and meet other children. When we were at North Berwick we sometimes drove over to a big farm, close to the sea. We enjoyed these visits tremendously for there were so many things to do and see. We rode the pony and saw the farmyard animals and walked along the lovely sands. There were rocks there too, and many ships were wrecked upon the jagged reefs until a lighthouse was erected upon the Bass Rock—designed by my father. Years afterwards I wrote a novel about this farm, about the fine old house and the beautiful garden, and I called it *The Story of Rosabelle Shaw*.

As we grew older we made more friends. We had bathing picnics and tennis parties and fancy dress dances, and of course we played golf. I was in the team of the North Berwick Ladies' Golf Club and I played in the Scottish Ladies' Championship at Muirfield and survived until the semi-finals. I was asked to play in the Scottish Team but by that time I was married and expecting my first baby so I was obliged to refuse the honour.

Every Spring my father and mother took us abroad, to France or Switzerland or Italy. We had a French maid so we spoke French easily and fluently—if not very correctly—and it was very pleasant to be able to converse with the people we met. I liked Italy best, and especially Lake Como which seemed to me so beautiful as to be almost unreal. Paris came second in my affections. There was such a gay feeling in Paris; I see it always in sunshine with the white buildings and broad streets and the crowds of brightly clad people strolling in the Boulevards or sitting in the cafés eating and drinking and chattering cheerfully. Quite often we hired a carriage and drove through the Bois de Boulogne. My sister and I were never allowed to go out alone, of course, nor would our parents take us to a play—as I have said before they were old-fashioned and strict in their ideas and considered a "French Play" an unsuitable form of entertainment for their daughters—but in spite of these annoying prejudices we managed to have quite an amusing time and we always enjoyed our visits to foreign countries.

In 1913 I "came out" and had a gay winter in Edinburgh. There were brilliant "Balls" in those far off days, the old Assembly Rooms glittered with lights and the long gilt mirrors reflected girls in beautiful frocks and men in uniform or kilts. The older women sat round the ballroom attired in velvet or satin and diamonds watching the dancers—and especially watching their own offspring—with eyes like hawks, and talking scandal to one another. We danced waltzes and Scottish country dances and Reels—the Reels were usually made up beforehand by the Scottish Regiment which was quartered at Edinburgh Castle. It was a coveted honour to be asked to dance in these Reels and one had to be on one's toes all the time. Woe betide the unfortunate girl who put a foot wrong or failed to set to her partner at exactly the right moment!

The First Great War put an end to all these gaieties—certainly nobody felt inclined to dance when every day the long lists of casualties were published and the gay young men who had been one's partners were reported dead or missing or returned wounded from the ghastly battlefields.

In 1916 I married Major James Reid Peploe. His family was an Edinburgh family, as mine was. Curiously enough I knew his mother and father and his brothers but had never met him until he returned to Edinburgh from the war, wounded in the head. When he recovered we were married and then began the busiest time of my life. We moved about from place to place (as soldiers and their wives and families must do) and, what with the struggle to get houses and the arrival—at reasonable intervals—of two sons and a daughter I had very little time for writing. I managed to write some short stories and some children's poems but it was not until we were settled for some years in Glasgow that I began my literary career in earnest.

Mrs. Tim was my first successful novel. In it I wrote an account of the life of an Officer's wife and many of the incidents in the story are true—or only very slightly touched up. Unfortunately people in Glasgow were not very pleased

with their portraits and became somewhat chilly in conse-
quence. After that I wrote *Miss Buncle's Book* which has
been one of my most popular books. It sold in thousands
and is still selling. It is about a woman who wrote a book
about the small town in which she lived and about the reac-
tions of the community.

All the time my children were growing up I continued to
write: *Miss Buncle Married, Miss Dean's Dilemma, Smoul-
dering Fire, The Story of Rosabelle Shaw, The Baker's
Daughter, Green Money, Rochester's Wife, A World in
Spell* followed in due succession—and then came the Second
Great War.

Hitherto I had written to please myself, to amuse myself
and others, but now I realised that I could do good work. *The
English Air* was my first novel to be written with a purpose.
In this novel I tried to give an artistically true picture of
how English people thought and felt about the war so that
other countries might understand us better, and, judging
by the hundreds of letters I received from people all over
the world, I succeeded in my object—succeeded beyond my
wildest hopes. My wartime books are *Mrs. Tim Carries On,
Spring Magic, Celia's House, Listening Valley, The Two
Mrs. Abbotts, Crooked Adam* and *The Four Graces*. In these
books I have pictured every-day life in Britain during the
war and have tried to show how ordinary people stood up
to the frightfulness and what they thought and did during
those awful years of anxiety. One of my American readers
wrote to me and said, "You make us understand what it
must be like to have a tiger in the backyard." I appreciated
that letter.

Wartime brought terrible anxieties to me, for my elder
son was in Malta during the worst of the Siege of that
island and then came home and landed in France on D-Day

and went through the whole campaign with the Guards Armoured Division. He was wounded in ten places and was decorated with the Military Cross for outstanding bravery. My daughter was an officer in the Women's Royal Naval Service and was commended for her valuable work.

In addition to my writing I organised the collection of Sphagnum Moss for the Red Cross and together with others went out on the moors in all weathers, wading deep in bog, to collect the moss for surgical dressings. This particular form of war-work is described in detail in *Listening Valley*.

After the long weary years of war came victory for the Allies, but my job of writing stories went on. I wrote *Mrs. Tim Gets a Job, Kate Hardy, Young Mrs. Savage* and *Vittoria Cottage*. All these books were quite as successful as their predescessors and *Young Mrs. Savage* was chosen by the American Family Reading Club as their Book of the Month. My new novel *Music in the Hills* is in the same genre and all those who have read it think it is one of my best. A businessman, who lives in London, wrote to me saying '*Music in the Hills* is as good as a holiday and, although I have read several other books since reading it, the peaceful atmosphere lingers in my mind. I hope your next book will tell us more about James and Rhoda and the other characters for they are so real to me and have become my friends." The scene of this book is laid in the hills and valleys of the Scottish Borders and the people are the rugged individualistic race who inhabit this beautiful country. For a long time it has been in my mind to write a story with this setting and to try to describe the atmosphere, to paint an artistically true picture of life in this district. Now it is finished and I hope my large and faithful public will enjoy reading it as much as I have enjoyed writing it.

Sometimes I have been accused of making my characters "too nice". I have been told that my stories are "too pleasant", but the fact is I write of people as I find them and am fond of my fellow human beings. Perhaps I have been fortunate but in all my wanderings I have met very few thoroughly unpleasant people, so I find it difficult to write about them.

We live in Moffat now. Moffat is a small but very interesting old town which lies in a valley between round rolling hills. Some of the buildings are very old indeed but outside the town there are pleasant residential houses with gardens and fine trees of oak and beech and elm. From my window as I write I can see the lovely sweep of moorland where the small, lively, black-faced sheep live and move and have their being. Every day the hills look different: sometimes grey and cold, sometimes green and smiling; in winter they are often white with snow or hidden in soft grey mist, in September they are purple with heather, like a royal robe. Although Moffat is isolated there is plenty of society and many interesting people to talk to and entertain and it is only fifty miles from Edinburgh so, if I feel dull, I can go and stay there at my comfortable club and see a good play or a film and do some shopping.

There are several questions which recur again and again in letters from friends and acquaintances. Perhaps I should try to answer them. The first is, why do you write? I write because I enjoy writing more than anything. It is fascinating to think out a story and to feel it taking shape in my mind. Of course I like making money by my books—who would not?—but the money is a secondary consideration, a by-product as it were. The story is the thing. Writing a book is the most exciting adventure under the sun.

The second question is, how do you write? I write all my books in longhand, lying on a sofa near the window in my drawing room. I begin by thinking it all out and then I take a pencil and jot it all down in a notebook. When that stage is over I begin at the beginning and go on like mad until I get to the end. After that I have a little rest and then polish it up and rewrite bits of it. When I can do no more to it I pack it up, smother the parcel with sealing wax, and despatch it to be typed. I am now free as air and somewhat dazed, so I ring up all my friends (who have been neglected for months) and say, "Come and have a party."

Another question is, do you draw your characters from real life? The answer is definitely NO. The characters in a novel are the most interesting part of it and the most mysterious. They must come from Somewhere, I suppose, but they certainly do not come from "real life". They begin by taking shape in a nebulous form and then, as I think about them and live with them, they become more solid and individualistic with definite ideas of their own. Sometimes I get rather annoyed with them; they are so unmanageable, they flatly refuse to do as I want and take their own way in an arbitrary fashion.

All the people in my books are real to me. They are more real than the people I meet every day for I know them better and understand them more deeply. It is difficult to say which is my favourite character, for I am fond of them all, but the most extraordinary character I ever had to deal with was Sophonisba Marks (in my novel *The Two Mrs. Abbotts*.) I intended her to be a subsidiary character, an unimportant person in the story, but Miss Marks had other ideas. In spite of the fact that she was plain and elderly and somewhat deaf and suffered severely from rheumatism, Miss Marks walked straight into the middle of the stage and stayed there. She just wouldn't take a back seat. She is so real to me that I simply cannot believe she does not exist. Somewhere or other she must exist—perhaps I shall meet her one day! Perhaps I shall see her in the street, coming towards me clad in her black cloth coat and the round toque with the white flowers in it and carrying her umbrella in her hand. I shall stop her and say loudly (because of course she is deaf) "Miss Marks, I presume!"

It will be seen from the foregoing sketch that my life has not been a very eventful one. I have had no hair-raising adventures nor travelled in little-known parts of the world, but wherever I have been I have made interesting friends and I still retain them. Friends are like windows in a house, and what a terribly dull house it would be that had no windows! They open vistas, they show one new and lovely views of the countryside. Friends give one new ideas, new values, new interests.

Thank God for friends!

Someday I mean to write a book of reminiscences; to delve into the cupboard of memory and sort out all the junk. There is so much to write about, so many little pictures grave and gay, so many ideas to think about and disentangle and arrange. Looking back is a fascinating pastime; looking back and wondering what one's life would have been if one had done this instead of that, if one had turned to the left at the crossroads instead of to the right, if one had stayed at home instead of going out or had gone out five minutes later. Jane Welsh Carlyle says in one of her letters, "One can never be too much alive to the consideration that one's every slightest action does not end when it has acted itself but propagates itself on and on, in one shape or another, through all time and away into eternity."

FICTION BY D.E. STEVENSON

* see Explanatory Notes

EXPLANATORY NOTES

Mrs. Tim

Mrs. Tim of the Regiment, the first appearance of Mrs. Tim in the literary world, was published by Jonathan Cape in 1932. That edition, however, contained only the first half of the book currently available from Bloomsbury under the same title. The second half was originally published, as *Golden Days*, by Herbert Jenkins in 1934. Together, those two books contain Mrs. Tim's diaries for the first six months of the same year.

Subsequently, D.E. Stevenson regained the rights to the two books, and her new publisher, Collins, reissued them in the U.K. as a single volume under the title *Mrs. Tim* (1941), reprinted several times as late as 1992. In the U.S., however, the combined book appeared as *Mrs. Tim of the Regiment*, and has generally retained that title, though a 1973 reprint used the title *Mrs. Tim Christie*. Adding to the confusion, large print and audiobook editions of *Golden Days* have also appeared in recent years.

Fortunately no such title confusions exist with the subsequent Mrs. Tim titles—*Mrs. Tim Carries On* (1941), *Mrs. Tim Gets a Job* (1947), and *Mrs. Tim Flies Home* (1952)—and Dean Street Press is delighted to make these long-out-of-print volumes of the series available again, along with two more of Stevenson's most loved novels, *Smouldering Fire* (1935) and *Spring Magic* (1942).

SMOULDERING FIRE

Smouldering Fire was first published in the U.K. in 1935 and in the U.S. in 1938. Until now, those were the only complete editions of the book. All later reprints, both hardcover and paperback, have been heavily abridged, with entire chapters as well as occasional passages throughout the novel cut from the text. For our new edition, Dean Street Press has followed the text of the first U.K. edition, and we are proud to be producing the first complete, unabridged edition of *Smouldering Fire* in eighty years.

FURROWED MIDDLEBROW

*titles available in paperback only

Made in the USA
Las Vegas, NV
14 September 2022